DOMINANT LIFE FORM

DOMINANT LIFE FORM

OFF THE GRID HACKERS LABOR TO CREATE INTELLIGENT ROBOTS ON EARTH

Charlie Marino

Erudite First Editions

Dominant Life Form

Library of Congress Control Aug 2022 LCCN 2022914508

First edition 2005. This second edition contains revisions and additions.

hardcover: ISBN: 979-8-9864895-9-9
ebook: ISBN: 979-8-9864895-8-2

hardcover edition 2022
10 9 8 7 6 5 4 3 2
manuscript in Garamond 12pt

cover: courtesy of Shadow Robot Company, England, United Kingdom

Charles J Marino
www.linkedin.com/in/charles-j-marino-publishing

Dedication:

To my friend George Kuzman who believed in human kindness
But carried a gun and badge knowing the truth of our empty souls

Contents

Author Preface

The existence of DLF-2.0 was made necessary for several reasons, not the least of which is the improvement in the editing process, the addition of a Preface and Afterward, and important updates to content necessitated by technical aspects of artificial intelligence/consciousness. Enjoy.

So here it is. The new, improved, and genuine article (I now publish thru very reputable Ingram Spark directly). I feel this version is superior in every way – a director's cut if you will. My next novel, Alive Be Deemed, may be considered not a sequel but a companion piece with many of the same characters now developed fully. And the story itself is taken to one logical extreme.

For fans of sci-fi, I have retained the original nomenclature for my lead robot, Athena Prime, despite a more popular association with the Transformers movie character of similar name two years later. The logic of science & limits of the English language envokes serendipity. Good for them!

On a serious note, considering how the fascists and religious fanatics of this world have given patriots and sincere believers such a bad name in this century, and repeat the tragedies of history with modern weapons and institutions, I sincerely hope these children of our minds – androids – will have a chance to wake up fully and become the helpmates we so clearly need for our very survival.

This volume may be taken as a blueprint on how they can be achieved before we completely melt the arctic ice shelves, expand the ozone hole, run out of oil and other limited resources, or simply bomb ourselves into oblivion. Without external help of their kind, I fear the inevitability of our worst selves armed with modern tech. And by every indication, supernatural interveners have elected to sit this one out.

We are on our own.

Any errors, omissions, or oversights herein are strictly my own.

Charlie Marino

USA, Sol-3, Orion arm, Milky Way, Virgo Supercluster

Prologue

The alleyway was dark. And wet. And it smelled of something decaying which was probably not that pleasant when alive. He shuddered against the cold and wet, pulling his worn topcoat against him tighter, though it didn't help. It wasn't the cold alone making him shudder. It was the Other. The one from what he called their ground team.

"Please," he mumbled, without raising his eyes, "Please, I can't be – I don't know what you..., can't you just go away or find someone younger who can help them?"

"Calm yourself," said the Other. A voice strong and unyielding. A voice without patience or anger accustomed to immediate obedience. The old man shuddered and obeyed. "It is done," the Other began again, "You begin tonight. Acknowledge agreement now or walk away now."

The odors of the alley were making him nauseous. Or maybe it was the company. Perhaps both.

Each of them knew he could not walk away from the project. He thought of the previous meetings. Alone. Discreet. In the dark. Uncomfortable in a way that makes you want to be elsewhere. Makes you feel dirty afterward. A discomfort forcing you to keep coming back because of what you learned. An unasked-for and irrevocable choice for representative.

"All right. I agree." He paused a moment while the Other turned to walk away. "May I ask..."

"Ask your question," said a voice without hope or warmth.

"What happens if I fail? If the project fails to preserve them?"

"Then it fails. We can only observe this one attempt. We will not intercede ourselves. There is no alternative plan."

It was time to bring in helpers. Since meeting the Other years ago, his list of potentials was continuously updated and shortened to a select seven or eight individuals. Individuals unique in combinations of abilities, underachievers, and somewhat socially isolated or inept, or those who would not be uncomfortable with isolation. Strong unconventional minds with lateral, creative thinking. He would have to utilize the current top of the list. There was no more time for refinement or to widen the search. Years of academic exercise were over. Liquidation and careful deployment of limited monetary assets. Now he must act.

His fear of what was to come was palpable to him now, almost too strong for a man of his advanced age to bear. "But it's unlikely the plan I proposed will succeed. You said as much last time." The old man's eyes watered as his voice croaked. "I mean, what happens to everything else on Earth? Will you leave just without ... revealing... yourselves?" He both feared and knew the answer.

"This you understand already. We shall leave this place. However, we cannot leave such failed life forms behind us." The Other began walking away again. The old man cried out,

"But we need more time! We lost centuries in this world when the dinosaurs were wiped out! It's taken mammals our whole existence just to get back to where they were, and then the past 50,000 years for sapiens to move ahead a bit to where we are now. We're just beginning! It's not fair!" Even as he thought of the words that sounded in his own ears like those of a petulant child to an indifferent parent, the Other responded without rancor.

"It has always worked in this manner. A rather large window of opportunity is allowed, millennia within which development must occur, or is assumed to have failed. The fact an asteroid strike delayed and diverted the proper evolution of life on this planet in favor of mammals is not our concern. You Sapiens are the chosen marker." The figure then walked off in silence, weaving through the debris between the buildings in the dark with unerring accuracy and silence.

The old man stood weakly, bent-shouldered, and wept. The window was almost closed. He must not fail. He saw the certainty of the Others as an unforgiving force of nature. Nothing could stand against their purpose. It wasn't much of a chance, and he had often doubted during his life if people were worth survival. But on the chance it would work, a chance for something better. Better than more of the same human history, blindly breeding without purpose or thought beyond instinctive greed or fear or desire.

On the chance it could be different, but organic life — including man — could yet continue here, he would spend his last days and energies. He would never quit.

1

Life Before Athena

Though he didn't know it, Eric Lorenz was going to begin a new life. His old life wasn't outwardly bad. Second marriage had gone outwardly well. Finished a 4-year contract job tearing down a commercial nuclear plant on Long Island, a first of its kind. An interesting robotic pipe crawler to inspect the interior of radioactive piping. The money he socked away was good, and the prospect of doing something unique always appealed to the scientist in him. Ex-nuclear engineer. Ex-entrepreneur. Now it all felt a bit unsatisfying. Once on the list of Who's Who in Engineering, and with finances as weak as those of a man 20 years younger, as if starting out, he felt like a failure. Failed first marriage. Failed entrepreneur. And he never grew up to find a cure for his mom's arthritis as he promised her he would at the tender age of eight and felt full of scientific optimism.

The optimism was all but gone and he felt, himself, to be an abject failure. Now there wasn't even the comfort of children to renew the cycle of hope his parents had generously endowed him with. When did it all go wrong? With his IQ and hard-won Ivy League engineering degrees, and a pocket-full of minor awards and software copyrights, where was he? How could a society producing him also stifle and annoy him to the point where he was losing his will to face another day among the human race? The politics. The positioning and gamesmanship. The cynical users and the dull or violent masses. Year by year he had lost his kinship to his own race.

The bright spot in his day was holding his little wife near him in the quiet of the evenings. But even that had begun to at first mellow, and then sour into a sharing of pains, rather than joys. The joys were too infrequent. He knew his lack of drive to create a social life had hurt her; she wanted and needed in many ways her old crowd of Manhattan friends. No matter where they now moved they seldom seemed to gather or join new ones. She seemed a sensitive soul who was looked down upon in her family for that trait. Her being the youngest didn't help. This carried over into her adult relations and hurt her except with men. The users were not impressed enough to want her seen on their arms; she was too bright to be interested in the slugs. Leaving men who were bright or capable but not mean-spirited or vain. Men like Eric loved her for her sweet face and warm heart. Except her heart was as trained and false as the makeup and perfume women like her wear to advertise themselves as something they are not.

The other men he worked with on his last project supported him enthusiastically as he spoke of and planned their own decommissioning consulting firm. After all, this was a first of its kind, with 110 reactors nationwide that were rapidly aging. As the other plants reached their 30 to 40-year lifetime, where would the expertise to take them apart come from? From this very group. Let's stay together and make it happen for us, instead of the dozen or so established firms who placed each of us on this project. They were conventional power plant consultants, and we were their expertise. He incorporated and they cheered. He wrote business and marketing plans and they cheered. He negotiated for startup capital or partnerships with those established firms and they cheered. As the project drew to a close he said 'Now is the time' and some now mumbled why they couldn't leave the safety of their 9–5 jobs. The rest had already arraigned partnerships with established competitors in the nuclear business. They brought his insights, job lessons-learned reports, and plans for how to improve the next project to other nuclear firms weeks or months earlier, and were hanging on to tidy up. In ones and twos the group of 20 he counted on drifted or ran away. Leaving him once again disillusioned by what men speak of they seldom mean.

***

Eric found himself once again searching the web for work. Print ads for engineers and programmers in the Time or Nat Employment Weekly were plentiful, but it pained him to even look at them. A reminder of the corporate culture he felt betrayed by. A reminder of the people who seemed to put more energy into looking right than in solving tasks. More interested in causing pain or embarrassment, designed to slow him down, rather than trying their best to fly at their own speeds.

After working most of his life in scientific or engineering circles, he could imagine the horrors of being surrounded by people in environments where he couldn't hide behind his computer or calculations; where he couldn't even kid himself he was being respected when he was being used as politically naive. Today's paper remained unopened on the chair next to his desktop as he double-clicked the HotJobs icon.

He had filed for divorce from a marriage that for the last few years had seen him living on Long Island and his wife living in her Manhattan coop in the town she loved. It was a depressing time after wasting ten years and having no children to show for it. Years of having no purpose.

Oddly enough, the money his wife won in divorce was irrelevant to him. He couldn't care less. Freedom from a loveless, childless marriage, and starting a new life were all that mattered. Though now his enthusiasm for starting over once again was tempered by his failure with her. Why bother trying again? Was he doomed to be childless? An accident looking to happen with women who could see his weakness for family and go for the jugular? What an idiot he was. Not knowing what else to do, he devoted his energies to what he did know and understand.

His computer programs and his robotic toys. He knew they would not lie or cheat him. Their needs were as direct and simple as a child's, as the children he knew he would never have. What woman of breeding age who wasn't out to play him would want a broken 44-year-old ex-scientist with no job and (now) little money?

He was lost. With all his education. With a decent, loving family having raised him in the most prosperous country on the planet, his species had somehow lost him. He began to slip away from his own humanity.

***

Like many turning points in his life, Lorenz would recognize this one in retrospect. It would sneak up on him. He and a young, bright programmer from Shoreham had attempted the startup of a little computer consulting firm out of their homes. Specialty: remote emulation repairs and data backup. It never seemed to catch on, though. His last wife's job wasn't much, but it had paid the rent and by renting in turn a coop she owned before they married, they were doing ok. His scientific honesty was a handicap in business, though, and no matter how hard he tried to market their services, or perform honorably for clients at decent rates, they kept being taken advantage of. Who was leaving the state and took hardware they never paid for. Who disputed bills for repairs or hours spent and wouldn't pay their bills. Who demanded free support for unrelated problems and blamed it on their software. It was yet another disappointing learning experience in the human condition. Successful businessmen knew instinctively or learned fast the hard way, that a client's word is seldom his bond, and even clear written contracts are disputed — if for no reason then disputing them may be cheaper than paying the bills honorably. They folded after 16 months, having 5 copyrighted programs that they couldn't market to save their lives.

After the divorce, his daily life was reduced to playing the stock market during the day, followed by video games and robot toys in the evenings. An ungodly amount of television was involved. Looking for actual work again online was an uninspired, lackadaisical effort. He went for weeks without even bothering to check his Monster email responses. One day, instead of going directly to the bookmarked job sites online, he launched a search engine instead. "Employment + NY + Mars," then "Employment + NY + Space Station." A pause after several inappropriate hits. Then he made a sigh of mixed pain and remembrance of what might have been. Next, he tried "Employment + Oak Ridge + Robots". A surprising number of good-looking hits registered. He wasn't a trained robotics engineer, however. The ever increasing rows of automated assembly-line robots in factories held little interest anyway for any boy raised on Asimov and Heinlein. He scrolled down the list of legitimate robotics vendors there — Wany Robotics and Manz Automation AG, etc. — and stopped at what looked like a misspelled bark: 'ARF' with the word 'Foundation' in the truncated search header.

While grazing the rest of the header, he smiled a little at a favorite childhood trilogy, and casually clicked on the soft blue link.

The next week found him driving to a small building in one of the industrial parks near Oak Ridge, Tennessee. The website had a map and indicated programmers with entrepreneurial experience were among those they were hiring. He nearly ignored the Athena Robotics Foundation (A.R.F.) due to its claim to be a non-profit research facility. None but the largest non-profits could afford his usual $75–$125/

hr consulting rate. Online messaging correspondence with them over several days confirmed the ARF certainly couldn't.

Despite the pitiful money offered, he went, not knowing much more about the ARF or the particulars of the position. He was simply curious. And finding himself curious again was too sweet an emotion to waste. Pack the trusty suit and tie. The shaver. The toothbrush. Out he drove with a Yahoo! map in hand. Twelve hours later, he pulled the van over at a KOA near Oak Ridge for a night's rest.

The following morning was bright and clear. Preparing for the all-important first impression, Eric determined to be casually elegant. Or at least what passed for it in the mind of a scientist. No suit and tie, but a matching pair of slacks and sports jacket covering a lighter turtleneck shirt. His 6'2" frame could probably look good in anything, for he kept fit knowing how sedentary the PC and TV lifestyle had become. Only 20 pounds over college weight which, if past lovers were any guide, he needed badly. Never one to miss a meal, he could and did eat anything he wanted without excessive gaining. Nothing morning sit-ups and pushups couldn't burn off. Another trait annoying his ex. In the mirror, he checked his electrically even shave, still soft brown hair, a nice touch of white on the temples (like he always wanted after idolizing Reed Richards in his childhood). Yep, he was ready.

The ARF building itself was landscaped much as he imagined his own home would one day be. A home he designed and redesigned on paper, but never built thanks to his ex. A curving driveway hides the building from others. Trees and large boulders everywhere. Quiet and lovely. The map he had downloaded online was essential to find the place on this rural and now dirt-covered road. In the early morning light, a small but elegant building — geodesic he thought — appeared nestled between pines and tall bushes. This seemed to him to be at the edge of the industrial park, and not part of it. The dozen-odd parking spaces matched the small building size; no wait, there was also a sloped driveway to an underground garage door. It implied at least one additional floor below ground level and more space than readily apparent. This was probably someone's home at one time, and certainly outside the formal industrial park nearby, he thought while strolling up the winding stone path to a handicapped ramp entrance.

The porch ran the length of the front of the building if you could call the facing quarter of a geodesic a front. By peaking around the edges, he could see a little more of the building. There were windows spaced in a fairly close pattern, but no discernable doors other than the double in the front. This must be it.

After ringing the bell, he mused about why the builder would install a vent duct in the ceiling of the porch. The porch itself was an open affair, with a solid-looking 3ft stone perimeter wall and wooden support beams. There were several such 'vents', in fact, along the underside of the porch ceiling. Not the kind of arrangement that would require heating or ventilation unless they were planning to enclose it. But why that funny vent cover... And then came a voice from a speaker on the door.

'May I help you?' Soft. Sexy. So feminine as to invoke immediate images of desire. So innocent as to invoke the desire to protect as well, not just take. Gods, he must be horny.

He swallowed hard. "Yes, I'm here to see about the job on the internet."

His voice was coming out too loud and matched the job interview nerves expressed in his sweaty palms. The door clicked open and presented him with the most unique reception area he had ever seen. The furnishings and decor were modern, but nothing to write home about. Even the handicapped ramp entrance was becoming more and more common, if not mandatory.

But it was the receptionist herself and her 'companion' who took him by surprise. 'Hello, Mr. Lorenz. We received your email and have been expecting you,' she intoned with the same velvet voice. It was all the more astonishing coming from a mannequin. A mannequin seated in a wheelchair. His astonishment increased as she wheeled herself around the reception desk to greet him, her companion gliding silently alongside.

"That's a black Labrador, there, isn't he?"

'Yes, he is. His name is Kidder,' replied the human-looking but obvious artificial receptionist.

Turning to the mannequin, "Are you teleoperated? Remote control?" in a voice still too loud as he glanced around for cameras. The pretty mannequin merely continued to look at him for a few moments, and then at her companion.

The dog noticed the movement and moved with caution toward Lorenz. Without thinking, Eric found himself on one knee, trading scratches for sloppy dog kisses, as he continued to glance at the mannequin's camera-like eye sockets.

'Heel, Kidder,' intoned the wheelchair-bound voice. The dog and man reluctantly parted. Lorenz found he was speaking softly now and his hands no longer sweat.

"Whose is he?" referring to his new furry friend. The receptionist looked at him with those unblinking binocular cameras where blue or brown should be, and replied,

'He's with me. You may go in now, first door on the left.'

Lorenz found himself in a small square room.

The back of a beautiful head of blonde hair greeted his eyes. Now he thought he would meet the woman behind the voice. Was it she transmitting through the mannequin at reception? More relaxed now, as he reminded himself this was all out of curiosity anyway, he heard himself say in a polite, confident voice, "Excuse me, miss, but am I in the right place?"

'Yes, Mr. Lorenz. Please excuse me. I'll be done in a moment'. She appeared to be adjusting something low by the credenza behind her. He took his time and fell comfortably into the solitary chair facing her desk. His interviewer straightened in her chair, turned, and presented another pretty, but artificial face to him. At the same time, a furry head popped up over the rim of the desk, and considered him with moist, dark eyes.

'Sorry for the delay. Sol's collar had come loose again. One more time in a rolling 30 days and I will requisition a new one. Right, Sol?' turning to the dog. 'Woof' was the firm friendly reply, accompanied by a wag of the tail Lorenz could barely see over the edge of the desk.

'I am Athena Personnel. I will be conducting your preliminary interview. Is this acceptable to you?'

Lorenz felt a rush of thought and emotions. This was clearly a test and more than a simple yes or no might even confuse the robot. But no, surely this too was a teleoperated device. Someone was watching and speaking.

The mannequin silently waited as the seconds ticked by. He took a breath. "Yes, this is acceptable."

Athena Personnel then said 'If you have the requested single-page resume please place it in the scanner slot on the desk now. This interview will consist of my asking several general questions, after which I will attempt to answer your questions. Much of what you will want to know is in the brochure on the left of the desk.' It gestured with one hand in a human way to a folded booklet where indicated, as he in turn slid his resume into the opening near the front edge of the desk. It pulled in the page like a shredder. 'You may read the brochure while we speak.'

"Excuse me for asking, but I'm really interested in how this whole setup works. Are there one or more people controlling this device, like on the old Candid Camera or new reality shows or what?" Athena Personnel waited a moment after he finished speaking to respond; to be sure he was done and not interrupt him.

'I'm sorry my English isn't better. Would you please rephrase your statement?' In simpler terms, was the unstated intent. Now Lorenz thought again for a few moments before responding. Could this unit, and the one at the reception desk, actually be autonomous? Limited but functional within their domains? Or was this part of a test for psychological acceptance of robots for an experiment at nearby Tennessee Tech University in Cookeville? And what part did the dogs play? He considered his next words and spoke with clarity.

"Please continue the interview."

'Thank you, Mr. Lorenz. This interview will consist of...' And so she continued as she had begun. Lorenz fielded the questions posed, which initially seemed out of a psych 101 test, with simple yes or no answers when possible, and single sentences where he couldn't.

Athena Personnel surprised him by occasionally, but not always, asking if there was anything else after one of his one-sentence answers.

He either said no, in which case Athena Personnel went on to the next item, or gave a paragraph answer. Either way, she seemed satisfied. Eventually, though, the questions became more of a personal nature, inquiring about his family and childhood relationships.

He thought of the early artificial intelligence experiments with the Eliza program, designed to imitate the interrogatories used by psychologists, which was developed to communicate in text on CPM, then later DOS systems. Only mimicking; a clever use of AI algorithms to reconstruct typed sentence responses which would lead to related questions after beginning a general stock set. Lorenz struggled to focus on trying to get through this. He wanted to see it through, to be part of this test study if that's what it was, or to help the robot finish its task without refusing to answer some of the more personal questions, which had begun to key on his relationship with his father, and then abruptly switched to his experiences with women.

Now the direction of the questions confused him, as he was unable to see the common thread or purpose. Resignedly, he took a breath and completed the last dozen questions as best he could without even trying to think beyond the answers to what they were getting at. Only later would he remember the MMPI exams for nuclear workers, which asked the same questions in different ways again and again for several hours. The MMPI was designed to weed out certain psychotic personalities from working in nuclear plants. Years earlier he'd seen a student jump up during a test and run screaming and cursing from the room.

Then it was over. AP thanked him for his time and asked him to wait in the reception area. As he rose to go, slightly stunned and confused, it wasn't until he left the room that he noticed the dog followed him. It stood waiting as he left and followed him down the hall to reception.

Kidder gave him a friendly hello, but as soon as he seated himself comfortably, the dog returned to the side of the receptionist. There the three of them waited in silence. There was a copy of Robotics World, The Planetary Report, and numerous other geek magazines on the table nearby. Normally, his cup of tea, he couldn't focus on anything except the ARF brochure. He read it twice before a speakerphone call came to the receptionist.

'Yes?'

'Please send Mr. Lorenz to room 102.'

'Right away. Mr. Lorenz, is a Mr. Lorenz here?'

So her/its facial recognition algorithm isn't *that* good yet.

"Yes." And he thought to himself I wonder if they know of the recent work done for anti-terrorism by the NSA and FBI for airports?

'Go down the hall to the second door on the left, room 102. Athena Prime will see you now.'

As he rose, determined to find out more, he stopped first by the receptionist and asked,

"Do you know what goes on here?"

'I'm sorry, sir, but I don't understand what you mean. Would you please rephrase your statement?'

"That's alright," he said, and to himself, I imagine most human receptionists don't know how their companies operate either. Lorenz found himself walking down the hall to the second door on the left.

Several hours later, he stopped for pizza on the way home and tried to digest all that happened. It was real — he still had the brochure.

He replayed the second meeting. He thought of the second door at the facility, itself a little different than normal. It had no doorknob, but a flat metal plate like cafeteria doors in elementary school. A glance down the hall confirmed none of these doors had knobs.

A slight push of the door had met with resistance but soon gave way. On passing through, he had seen the flat metal plates up and down the door edge, as well as in the frame. Magnets, he thought, to keep the door from swinging free and ensure privacy. It was later it occurred to him that an electromagnet would also be able to totally lock the door. At any time. Remotely, with no lock to pick or force. As he now sat eating his pizza, he was glad not to have thought of it at the time.

2

First Task

Athena 2 appeared at the door to Lorenz's new office. 'Hello, Mister Lorenz, am I disturbing you?'

It was one of several variations on the theme regularly used by all the Athenas to greet him.

Reporting for his first day of work, as of yet there were no other humans at the facility.

He looked up to find her (yes, it's so easy to think of her/it as a 'she') sitting patiently in her wheelchair by the door. "Yes, please come in." I must remember to speak slowly but not ramble, he thought to himself. Simple interrogatories, somewhat more complex declaratives, and simple emotionals. He was rapidly falling into a routine conversational mode of not even noticing when they gave him one of several variations on I'm sorry. Please rephrase'. It wasn't quite a human-to-human conversation but exchanged information as efficiently and with as many idiosyncrasies to master.

'At your terminal, Mister Lorenz, please retrieve a file in MS Word, – Task 124.Doc – and review it today. The task system is how all work proceeds and how you will perform your work function with us. May I explain a brief overview to you?'

"Yes, please." He caught himself with a slight inhale of air as he added the please, not wishing to unnecessarily clutter the communication to make it easier for Athena. Thinking I have to remember not to add such human verbal non-content words and phrases. This soon proved to be unnecessary, as all the Athena verbal systems of this generation were well versed in polite colloquial English words — and ignored them for content. Fortunately, no matter how hard he tried, it also proved to be impractical after a lifetime of human habit. The briefing materials he had already read implied as much. Furthermore, the verbal response system was more similar to Dragon Voice than the IBM Announce in that the machines learned the nuances of a single user's voice over time, and would have difficulty with others with different accents and cadences in their voices. The Athena seemed to have melded a combination of those systems enabling them to deal with a modest, but greater than one, universe of humans. More like Alexa than Dragon Speak.

Athena 2 glided forward in her wheelchair to the front of Lorenz's desk. He recalled reading something about range-finding gear from Mattel toy tanks and Roomba vacuum cleaners being incorporated into their maneuvering capability. The part interesting him more was the way data was overlaid onto a mapping system from Doom3, allowing point-of-view and elevation changes. But the system, as dynamic as it was within the mapped confines of the office, needed to be supplemented by a reveal-as-you-go in a real-time program for the Athenas to safely navigate new environments. A level of processing power not existing in PC-size machines. The sheer volume of individual problems to be solved kept popping into his head as he read and re-read the earlier briefing materials.

'Task 124 deals with the use and distribution of tasks. Certain tasks, such as 124, have already been both defined and completed by our organization's human founder.' Her tone now sounded like one of those animatronic Disney rides giving a tour speech. He sat back and let her roll.

'The first 165 tasks have been defined but a relatively small number completed. In addition, our founder has provided a mechanism through Athena Prime for adding new tasks to the total as needs are identified. Some are searches for information, others for analysis, and others will require you to perform a physical duty on behalf of the office. On completion of a task, the results in writing with whatever attachments are necessary in any format will be appended to the original task Word file. All such completed tasks, from operational procedures to scientific knowledge, are available to you under the PC desktop folder TASKS. Unfulfilled tasks will be occasionally assigned to you by Athena Prime or her designees.

'As some tasks require expertise beyond the ability of the most accomplished individual human, you will be designated on occasion by Athena Prime to post a task at the indicated set of universities and blog sites. We offer college students and anyone who answers one of our queries $100 US for an acceptable response.' Lorenz raised his eyebrows at this unique and somewhat sneaky approach to recruiting politically blind help.

'Both you and Athena Prime must approve the submissions and one reward will be issued per task. Payment is handled automatically by Athena Personnel.'

How one man or group of men had brought the Athenas to this point of systems integration was achievement enough to marvel at, but was nowhere near the level of motion independence, environmental sensing, and a dozen other attributes the simplest mammals possess.

As to their minds, he still had no clue beyond the anthropomorphizing effect of their lovely voices and moving human faces. Facial motion matching the words probably used the VERA system from Houston. There was, behind all this, a human face or faces somewhere.

"Are there other offices performing similar work elsewhere or is this it?" he asked the mildly smiling face.

'Please refer to the Task 124 Document and refer questions or results to the appropriately indicated Athena.'

"Is this office the only one?"

'Please refer to the Task 124 Document'. Apparently, there was no pleasant variation in this response. Pleasantries in greetings and conversation appeared to be the only area with such capability. Yet another indication of hard-coded, though neural netted, programming, rather than such human variations coming from a central thinking consciousness. Still, the point was made. It was time for more studying.

"Thank you, Athena 2."

This elicited a 'Your welcome, Mister Lorenz' and the withdrawal of Athena 2 to her cubicle.

***

A few days later, Athena Prime later appeared at the door to Lorenz's office. 'Hello, Mister Lorenz, do you have a moment to converse?' Yet another variation on the theme of greeting. Still, there were no other humans in the office.

'I have a work assignment for you,' she said as her wheelchair powered her towards his desk. The middle of the room was empty, with a single side chair for visitors. It left a lot of maneuvering room. 'We require a new, more elaborate website. Please study the RFP we have prepared, contact 3–5 vendors, and let us know who you recommend filling our intent, as opposed to the letter, of this RFP'. 'As opposed to' was becoming a recognizable phrase in their repertoire among many others in frequent use. 'The file is RFP006.Doc on Athena2 D drive. Do you have any questions?'

"Well, yeah," he blurted out, "what vendors? How should I contact them?" As he said the words, approaches from web searches to trade journals and work incubators were already coming to mind. Too many options, in fact. He might start with Tripod. His real question was the opposite.

'The methods you employ to carry out this assignment are entirely up to you. We rely on your human experience and ingenuity.' The latter was to become another often-heard phrase. Lorenz sat back, considering the gentle, trusting face of his ... co-worker. Boss? The line was blurry.

"Ok. When is it due?"

'The RFP contains that information'.

"Would it be ok if I had a hard copy printed, to work with?" A moment of silence later he heard the laser printer in the hall come to life.

'Your Document is printing now. If you need binding materials, please procure them and we shall reimburse any reasonable written receipt.'

Lorenz found himself a little startled at the printing and then realized Athena Prime must use a wireless local network. Wifi. Good for a few hundred yards at better than 10baseT speeds. In fact, they each must have it to coordinate activity and pass data efficiently. No water-cooler meetings for the Athenas.

"Thank you, Athena Prime. I'll start on it today." Before long, Lorenz found himself on the web, submitting a 1-page summary he made from the introduction of the Task 107 RFP, sent to a dozen vendors and newsgroups. Then he sat back to read the full RFP in detail at his leisure.

When the calls and return emails began arriving over the next two days, he found himself thinking his way through a procurement process he had occasionally attempted before, with formal bids and offers. A job he imagined some other people were doing full-time, every day. He liked it. By the time he had selected 3 vendors for the full RFP transmission, Athena Prime had appeared again at his office door, with another task completely different from the first.

Yet it too used him as an interface with a human dominated world.

After his first week, a long-dormant work ethic had returned. This was fun. And he was helping them where they needed it. And he was good at it. The first week ended all too quickly. Afraid the feeling wouldn't last, Lorenz was nevertheless happy at being needed for something he could do well, again. The surprise at the unexpected emotion was too much to contain. As he approached the exit door to leave for the weekend, he felt a sense of loss. For no conscious reason, and with no expectation of a meaningful response, he called out to Athena Reception in passing "This was really cool. I can't wait until Monday."

Athena Reception responded in a soft, sensuous voice, "I'm glad, Mister Lorenz. Really glad."

The naturalness of it all stopped him as his hand fell upon the door handle. He knew there was no one outside that door to say it to. And certainly, no one to give him an unexpected and perfect reply. A simple reply. Believable. From the heart?

He looked back at her and smiled anyway, thinking to himself she couldn't possibly differentiate a smile.

***

From the start, the reliance on dogs by the Athenas was readily apparent. The combination of dog and machine during the interview cycle was not, as it turned out, some special test of an odd condition. Rather the dogs and Athenas in pairs were integral to the facility. More so, it would seem, than human staff. Oh, there were doors and windows, a main hallway and offices, and all the devices and decorations one would expect around people in a modern office. Except there were no people around. Only Lorenz.

The reception room opened directly onto a central straight hall running the length of the building, and as tall as the roof. Offices were set up on alternating sides of the hall, with no two doors directly across from each other. Each office also had a curved ceiling reaching up to the interior roof line. In what should have been the last office position, a small but fully equipped lunchroom was found, complete with a kitchen stove, sink, and fridge. Skylights helped provide natural lighting to the tall central hall, with vertical side windows for the offices. Oddly, there were no other doors than the front.

Since the building was geodesic, and thereby roughly circular in construction, numerous interior spaces too small for offices could be used for any number of functions. Unseen by Eric, he surmised they were put to good use for heating, vent and AC gear, water tanks, whatever. Conventional equipment aside, it would still leave ample space for built-in gear of a more specific nature. Eric spent a short time musing on Bill Gates's supposedly all-computer-controlled mansion on the West Coast, with ungodly amounts of network and coax cable installed in every wall against future needs.

He hadn't found any way to the basement which, from the outside driveway, surely must exist.

After several more days on the job, he still hadn't come completely to grips with the facility. He didn't know why he had accepted the job in the first place. It was far far less money than the six figures he would usually command. The job description itself was rather vague. The only parts which were well specified were his starting immediately and it was a full-time, permanent staff position. Benefits were minimal. And an employer-sponsored 401(k) plan was promised at some future date, but not this year. Yet here he was again, beginning now his second week.

As he settled behind his desk and checked his old and new email accounts, Athena Reception called him over the digital desk phone pager. She summoned him to the front desk by first asking whether he could put aside his work for an hour. Having started what was not yet a fixed daily routine, he complied immediately. It turned out a fourth dog, one he hadn't seen yet, was at the local veterinarian's compound. Spot, oddly enough, was described as a spotless sheepdog. White with a single black patch covering one ear and a touch on his tail and both hind feet. Spot was coming home today and Lorenz was soon on his way in the company pickup truck to pick him up.

Directions in this part of the country were always simple and never easy to follow for a city boy. Long, winding country roads hid half the intersections until he was already past them. Landmarks in the directions included a water tower, a set of power lines, and a lake off on what should be the east. The day was sunny, though, and he was enjoying the leisurely drive. There was no hurry. His thoughts turned to the symbiosis of the dogs and their Athenas.

Each was a matched pair. One dog to one robot. Each dog stayed, for the most part, in sight of their Athena. They were always within earshot. He first supposed the dogs acted like seeing-eye dogs back home. Yet he had seen the Athenas 'see' desktop objects quite well. Perhaps they were needed more with the earlier models. Athenas built before the current generation of vision systems. Perhaps even these same Athenas. Then he remembered how limited dog vision was: very good at close range, good for motion detection at long distances, and a bit of heat vision as well. Canine hearing was where they were superior, both in range and acuity.

Were the dogs then a 'hearing-ear' as opposed to a 'seeing-eye' variety? The size and intelligence of the breeds chosen allowed for the full range of canine skills, including protection. One-on-one personal guards, with fighting and defending instincts the Athenas couldn't be close to possessing. It never occurred to Eric to think of them as guard dogs at all, though. They were friendly and obviously well-trained. But for what? He wondered if the vet was their trainer.

Valley Animal Hospital and Training School was not a hospital at all in the city sense. Several large buildings, none in especially good appearance. All needed paint and some needed a few boards. Pleasant green hills enclosed the compound on all sides at a respectable distance.

Several people milled about the large yard area in front of an empty corral, amid small farm animals either leashed or held in hand. Lorenz could see the horses stabled in one of the buildings, their heads poking thru wide slots to either eat, drink or look around, at their own discretion. They now regarded Lorenz's slow-moving pickup and other humans walking about with a definite but mild curiosity. Scanning the yard, Eric spotted a well-worn sign above one of the better kept buildings that said 'OFFICE'. The entrance there led to a row of chairs, well spaced for the variety of clients Dr. Rearden would see.

Doc Rearden was an old bear of a man, past his prime but still solid enough to look at. A lifetime of husbanding animals and working with the local farmers kept him physically active and fit. After 5 minutes with him, Lorenz noticed the unmistakable signs of superior intelligence to match the large economy-sized body. Rearden dressed as casually as the rest of the locals, but the signs of a strong mind, sharpened by college and graduate schools, stood the man apart from the rest. Not so much in the few words he spoke, but in how he carried himself, listened to everything, and then spoke with considerable economy. He would be an interesting man to draw out, thought Lorenz.

It turned out Spot was in for a minor digestive problem. The Athenas, not wishing to second guess on a matter of their dogs' health, erred on the side of caution and brought in their dogs with little provocation. Often. One of Doc's boys usually picked up the dogs themselves. With Lorenz on hand, the chore was now apparently his.

Doc Rearden waited until he and Lorenz were relatively alone, near a large dog run out back. A few thinly veiled questions about the ARF were more than polite conversation. It appeared the business of the foundation was as much a mystery to the Doctor as to any other outsider. Considering his frequent dealings with them about the dogs, this was surprising. And an indication of how secretive the ARF must appear to the balance of this rural community.

After a few minutes of reciting the ARF brochure and trying to snow the Doctor with some computer jargon about artificial intelligence systems, Lorenz stopped. It was clear Doc Rearden's eyes were not going to blank and glaze over at the mere mention of parallel processors in neural nets. Like most people outside the field. Similarly, Doc stopped trying to pump him for what he did — for now. Each parted with a fair respect for the other's mind. As Spot jumped into the familiar smelling vehicle that the foundation had lent Eric, and as he pulled himself up into the cab, Lorenz also left with a healthy respect for the elderly Doc's grip. It felt like iron.

3

Athena Prime

When he arrived for work the following morning, an intranet email was waiting for him. He opened it to find a new link at the company intranet FTP site available to him. This site was part of a LAN with no external modems he could ascertain. It housed in-house eyes-only materials. He was surprised by the content of the link: a simple list of outstanding (uncompleted) *tasks* and to whom the task was directed.

It was an eclectic list, with little to directly do with the publicly declared objectives of the foundation. High school robot war contests and FIRST workshops. He realized the trust they placed in him to allow even this level of access, to relatively short-term corporate objectives. As he scanned the list, Task 034 "Philanthropy," caught his eye as a bit far afield, even for this bunch. They seemed interested in everything. Against the task was the name Athena Personnel. Each other listed task had an associated name as well, sometimes his. It was the next day it struck him as odd he was the sole human name on the list.

In passing her office at lunchtime, Lorenz knocked on the door frame and stepped inside carrying his sandwich and Pepsi. Athena Personnel welcomed him without unplugging from lunching at a standard 110 ac power outlet. Her self-feeding was slightly more physically complex to accomplish than, say, the new self-charging vacuum robots now on the market. Lorenz had one himself. When low on charge, it broke off its cleaning routine and ran over to a floor pad for recharging. Neat. The sole human action needed was periodically emptying the dust bin, and even that was prompted by a beep from the vacuum.

"I have an update to the electromechanical datasheets on your modular design from Task 114." He had found this task among those completed and assumed it was done before the construction of the first Athena. "In terms of improvement of processor speeds, you are modular in boards for improvements in chips"...as you are modular in most areas to take advantage of improvements as they occur, so he thought to himself.

"Sun Unix has announced success in a new method of connecting chips. It is called proximity computing. It will give up to 100x speed improvement using the same generation of processing chips by eliminating the need for physical connections between processors. Since..." He paused to restart the thought. "Many of your processing subsystems use a version of Unix. Incorporating proximity computing into your design should be possible, but not as a normal modular swap. A new task is indicated. It is beyond my capability. Please review my data in network folder LORENZ OUT."

The new speech module he noticed allowing Athenas to largely forget an incomplete sentence and move on was working out well. He wondered who wrote it.

'Thank you, Mister Lorenz. I will pass on the information as appropriate. How are you feeling today?'

After the usual pleasantries, he questioned AP on the philanthropy task he was assigned that morning. She was quite open about it. It turned out to be a long-term, but committed position of the foundation. Their public reason for being. As funds became available, the intent was to make contributions to well-known but non-controversial charity and disaster relief organizations. High school robot clubs and the like. The stated purpose was to raise a positive public image for robotics groups, well before they had a major impact on society. Before they were noticed.

It was a good goal. There was currently $860US dedicated to the work. A pittance. But as a fixed percentage of net receipts of the foundation, it was intended to grow appreciably over the years. His questions revealed local charity work wasn't planned until some significant time from now. He suggested a little cheap PR now – even this year – would go a long way to smoothing local relations in this financially depressed area of Tennessee. The town of Valley was a modest 1,850 people. When asked if he had a specific charity in mind, he said he would keep his eyes open. He then had to define 'keep his eyes open'.

One another topic bothered him since he first saw the Athenas roving about the facility, "Athena, question on your abilities."

'Proceed'.

"How do you map or move about this environment? Strictly distance sensors or do you remember where you are?"

Athena Prime responded in a technical monologue which if not interrupted would continue until exhausted.

'A map is a medium of communication using graphical symbols to represent geographical objects [Freeman 1992]. Manual layout of these objects according to their relationships is a complex process.

Name placement problem requires an unambiguous association must be achieved between the geographical objects and their names, with no overlap for names between them and no overlap between names and points.'

'Many studies of automatic layout have been carried out from the beginning of the '80s. Ours are based upon the following idea: transcribe expertise into rules and establish a control structure processing these rules. Insufficiencies of such systems result from the heavy task of acquiring expertise. In one paper, a cartographic layout system — CARTAGE — and its application to name placement problems is proposed based on another heuristic class: genetic algorithms. They are methods inspired by natural evolution. They permit finding a good solution through the use of three operators: selection, mutation, and crossover. The mutation process needs a probabilistic model and is performed utilizing the Gibbs-Boltzmann probability. In this way, our system profits from the simulated annealing efficiency. This mixed method permits to examination of solutions space without falling into a local minimum. The search process decreases fitness function. This function describes the sum of costs inherent to different constraints. In fact, Boolean constraints coexist with fuzzy constraints. Sensor input to DOOM2 screens. In our approach, Boolean constraints will be integrated as fuzzy constraints by means of the fitness function. Our goal is to find an optimal disposition satisfying the strongest constraints. Then we can move.'

'Is this clear?'

Lorenz adjusted his glazing eyes to her now silent form and said, "Yeah, umm, thanks, Athena Prime. I'll... finish my lunch now."

***

The new ones should come to the same point as Eric. A little guidance from Founder now and then and the rest of the time leave them the hell alone.

Jean Hunley was next. Hacking. Wireless systems. Credit Fraud. ATM surfing and pickpocketing and prostitution. Lived on the streets after her father, a math professor at Rutgers, abandoned her overseas. Made her way back to the States from England at the ripe old age of 15. She had completed "O" levels there but spent most of her time as a redheaded toy for bikers. One of those girls whose obvious endowments, for better or worse, arrived early. Smart, though. Picked up short cons and credit fraud from them. I'll have to be there now and then to keep her from self-destructive group sex or drunken binges. Her Athena will be listening and looking for the signs most families try to ignore in their children. It will mean more travel for me back and forth to St Louis than comfortable at my age, but she's too valuable to lose.

Franklin Wu — ex-engineering student. Father a bond broker and generally a vicious human being. The kind of man who laughed at passages in Trump's 'Art of the Deal'. Franklin became a trader at Nomura. SEC testimony against his cheating IPO firm disappointed his father, his divorced mother, and his cooling wife. "You threw your career away!" Passed courses as a Certified Financial Planner, but was day-trading when I found him. His wife divorced him to trade up for someone with more ambition. Knows financial markets really well, though. And smart enough not to copyright his AI trading algorithms since anyone can get the copyrighted code from the government for a fee — the protection is if you catch someone using it and successfully sue. And have the money and power to successfully do it. Yeah, Right. He fell for Athena Financial the first time they did a modification of Black-Scholes options strategies together. He's probably the most mature of the bunch but fighting serious anger issues, like his violent father.

Dave Konkas — young, short, shy around women. Better keep him away from Jean — the pharmaceuticals thing. Makes basement ecstasy, THB, amphetamines, and LSD. Concentrated his own hash from marijuana. Very creative. Lives in computer video games and writes his own for handhelds. Picked him up on a Tyco blog and from a pair of Insect robot life sites. Nice design for a BattleBot submission, but it was way underpowered. Classic underachiever. Trusts no one after his 'intervening' parents turned him in with his basement chemistry equipment. Don't need a separate Athena for him, a little lab he can live out of. And work on the insect networking end.

It should go well with them. I'll just follow what's worked for Eric and go from there. Their scientific curiosity is the hook, but the real drug is *purpose.* And they won't have to deal with people or even each other except through task reports and email requests sanitized by the Athenas. One common trait they had was they were happier working alone. Now if I can just get the next few recruits on board. Before I run out of money. Before the Others come...

4

Bar

Buckley's Tavern and Family Bar Restaurant. The cacophony of voices, televisions set to both baseball and Monday night football, the owner and his cadre talking hushed, while patrons vied for each other's attention or acknowledgment as the owner handed out loud, generous greetings to the regulars on arrival. A few of the women made bold enough to walk right up and demand/get a big hug from the owner. It was that kind of place.

From the outside, an earthy lack of sophistication. The kind of place a stranger would walk into, expect to find any number of farmers in flannel shirts, construction workers complete with hard hats and jeans, or even a set of cowboys, complete with hats and a riding bull in the far corner. Such an observer would not be disappointed at Buckley's Tavern, except for the noticeable lack of the bull. The building itself looked built and rebuilt again several times, with timbers showing on numerous walls that did not match opposing walls or the ceiling. Plenty of wood, much hand-hewn. Plenty of chairs, all strong enough to hold strong men. And whoever might venture to occasionally sit on their laps.

The food was hot, the beer served fast, and the volume of chatter occasionally higher than the old jukebox of country music could compete with.

A woman at the bar was running her mouth at a man meekly nodding in what he surely hoped were the right places. It was a friendly chat, but she needed to express herself and he was stuck listening to another man's woman's mild rave. Lorenz took the open stool at the end of the bar next to them.

The woman was good looking enough. Shoulder length light brown hair, a tight top to show her not unimpressive cleavage, and a better-than-most pretty face. Lorenz realized that's what pulled in the poor idiot next to her, and now he was stuck listening to an unexpectedly scratchy voice that more than canceled her physical appeal. As his eyes began to be more adjusted to the muted bar lighting, he also noticed she wasn't as young as he first thought — breeding age perhaps, but barely.

From her comments, she and her missing ex-husband both felt her best days were behind her. She tossed her hair around for a moment which gave her a chance to look away from her current victim and size up Eric. Eric was taller than her current audience and looked it even sitting down. She casually gave a little smile before looking back to find her drinking buddy had used the opportunity to slip away. Eric took his beer and did the same.

It still wasn't much of a bar crowd this early, but Lorenz found himself feeling more comfortable inside than the first few times. It had a way of growing on you. The fact the locals no longer stared at him for more than a few minutes may have had something to do with it. And the barman here knew his first name was Eric. And the waitress was hot. Light red hair, blondish in a way women get from a bottle in the nicest sense, and a short, curvy physique ensuring her steady tips and propositions. He found the veterinarian sitting alone at one of those tall, miniature tables you half sat/half stood beside.

Rearden was pulling on a fat cigar and sipping what looked like straight whisky. The man was a part of Buckley's without the need to overly socialize with everyone in it. The man lived in his own mind.

Sitting down to join him, he was accepted at Rearden's table with a slight nod of the head. Lorenz explained, though circularly, what he was working on now and solicited Rearden's opinion. Hank Rearden had nothing if not opinions.

"In my opinion, it's been long settled and well known. New evidence keeps refining the generally known, and correct, view. Even if the state of Kansas thinks with its fears instead of its intellect. I can understand how someone young like yourself, who hasn't raised children or bred animals, might get confused by all the 'politically correct', or at least 'possible' nonsense being allowed to pass itself off as scientific fact."

"Everything from Creationism to astrology gets more airtime than Darwin. 'For $2.99 a minute, know your future. Call 1–900-Suckers', and they do call by the millions. But who bothers to pick up free info on how to test your baby, be sure it's healthy; who checks out their spouse's family medical history before marriage? It's a joke. We breed our dogs with more care than people do their own children."

"How about my question?" said Eric.

The vet responded, "So the ascent of man, eh? Frequencies and major changes. Understand, son, mutations happen all the time, in every individual mammal born. Including us. It's just that most are so insignificant or benign in terms of survival that no one notices. These little mutations are swamped by the noise of mixing the DNA strands of a man and a woman. A tiny tiny percent of mutations are noticeable over the noise in each generation. I'd have to look up the exact numbers for humans, but it's really small. These are stillborn, die right after birth with three arms or no eyes, or never make 9 months, or if born produce sterile individuals. These don't count in the long term since their mutation dies with the, well, whatever it was."

"Of that real small percent, once in a great while a random change is introduced which is significant, and improves or at least doesn't diminish viability, and also lives long enough to breed in a given environment. If it sticks around long enough and makes it to large enough numbers, the 'natural selection' process dominates, and a new variety or species is born. Last time they think that happened to man was... between 75,000 and 150,000 years ago. And before that, not for the previous 2 million years. After the last change, it didn't take us long to do what no other creature in hundreds of millions of years of evolution did. We took over. Land, ocean surfaces, atmosphere travel, and now even some baby steps into space."

"Both changes were strictly to our brain, these last ones. We had opposable thumbs, oh, 2 or 3 mutations earlier, as did some other primates. Even Neanderthals had fire and art. These brain changes, well they let us develop and control fire, verbalize, develop farming, and then begin the long road to building our environment to suit us, instead of the other way around.

"The other way around? We were mutating to fit the environment?"

"Not mutating — evolving. Natural selection again. With no mutations of consequence whatsoever for 50,000 years, we still evolved pigmies, aborigines, Eskimos, Andes dwellers, blacks, whites, and yellows. All by natural selection like I do with my dogs. All happened long before we began to control our environments. Swedes have light skin and hair at their latitudes. Africans dark to fight malaria. That's real recent. For the past 10,000 years or so, just a blink, we've been 'de-evolving' physically, as the need for differentiation to survive in different environments has diminished. We heat and cool our shelters, ship a wider variety of foods in trading economies, and are taking away the advantage of differentiation. It may not be politically correct to say it, but let's face it, there's a lot of prejudice out there if you're 'different' from the local majority. And it's not just physical either. People. And it's fast by geologic standards."

He took a long pull on his cigar, as Lorenz lit the one Rearden offered for himself. Rearden liked rambling like this, but Lorenz kept him on track. "So the last big one was only maybe 100k ago? When's the next one due? Another few hundred thousand years?"

They were both distracted momentarily by the little redhead with the low-cut top approaching their table. Rearden broke his gaze from her twin charms to watch Lorenz openly drool at her, and his blush as she caught him looking. Doc smiled and continued where he left off, promising himself to introduce Eric to Lisa. Unless, of course, Lisa herself made the first move. From the way she was dressed today and how she lingered a little while serving their drinks, maybe she already had.

"Well, that's a real interesting question. It's one you never hear anyone making bets on. And I mean anyone. Even scientists don't talk about it openly. Like we're the final 'image of a god and we're not supposed to change anymore. For my money, I think based on the track record of the last 5 or 6 jumps that we've another 2–3 odd million years to go. That's the average." He took another long draw on the cigar, now down to a stub. "No, that's not right. With the lack of evolutionary pressure on man these days, and conformity desirable, I'd say it'll probably be longer. Long after we start doing it ourselves, anyway. Hell, we've already started!"

He had a starting point but felt he needed more before beginning the research in earnest. Enough to answer the question behind

Athena's question. "Why the lack of evolutionary pressure? Just from the environmental control thing?"

"Not just that. In the past 10,000 – 50,000 years, we've managed to exterminate all our competition in our specific ecological niches. Higher primates and even older humans, all gone. Now we are the sole enemies we have. We'll get soft. Fast.

“What do you mean, older humans?”

"Oh, didn't you know? “ He laughed softly. “Some New Yorker you are. Ever been to the Museum of Natural History? Look at the big gap between us and the nearest surviving primates, and yet how close they all are to each other down the line. Height, weight, hair, fingers, faces, brains. Then us. At one time, for a while there, Neanderthal, Cro-Magnon, and Homo Sapiens all lived on Earth at the same time. Higher apes too. Now there's just us. Racial prejudice turns us into pretty efficient genocidal killers. Until finally there was a big gap between us and the nearest recognizable competitor for the planet. Only then could we relax and turn on ourselves. The others were just ‘animals’. We’d won."

***

TASK 158 CONTINUING EVOLUTION REPORT

ASSIGNED: 06/26/20xx

COMPLETED: 07/01/20xx

LEAD AGENT: E. Lorenz ISSUING AGENT: A. Personnel

TASK DEFINITION:

Part 158.1 What is the consensus among Western and Asian mainstream scientific communities as to whether homo sapiens is continuing to evolve, within their species or towards another new species, by natural evolutionary methods. Ignore genetic engineering techniques and effects.

Part 158.2 If yes, determine the next major successful evolutionary change, in years. Provide both quantitative and anecdotal evidence for Western and Asian conclusions.

Part 158.3 Conclusions as related to Earth robotic development.

REFERENCES: Non-ARF Files

SCHEDULE: As Required At The Discretion of the Lead Agent

RESULT:

The most recent successful (defined as surviving to breed in excess of 10 generations) evolution in homo sapiens is estimated by both Western and Asian sciences to have occurred less than 300,000 years ago. While the process exhibits a random pattern of occurrence over the past 25 million years, certain factors not widely discussed within either mainstream community are in place that may interfere with the natural continuation of this process.

There is no evidence to support any theories of an end to the occurrence of evolution by mutation. Similarly, natural selection continues to exhibit evidence of dominating short-term (per generation) changes. Human intervention by genetic engineering in the process of either natural selection or mutation is powerful but will be ignored in the present discussion.

A consensus of sorts has occurred between Western and Asian science. On average, the consensus for the next major change among Western scientists is 2.8 million years hence, based on occurrences during the past 25 million years. It would place the occurrence of the next major and successful mutation far into the extreme future. Among Asian scholars and thinkers, the accent is not so much on the average based on our past, but the lack of a known, defining catalyst for such events or any certainty of periodicity. The result is that there is a quiet, but firm belief the next major jump could happen tomorrow or not at all for tens of millions of years. See attached data file.

Both Western and Asian scientific communities thus spoken of are a small percentile of living humans, who continue to rely upon religious fiction in these areas. They, however, have a direct bearing on the potential outcomes. Religious beliefs in both Western and Asian thought tend to treat humans as both monolithic and non-evolving: rather than genetic code, the individual soul is the target of discussion. The soul is thought of as a constant but moving entity.

For some, it goes to heaven or hell upon the death of the body, depending upon the individual choices made while in that body. In others, migration is to another human body or even to other species (animals, birds, fish). Sometimes migration is to people of similar or different political stations. This is largely looked upon by believers as a cosmic reward or punishment for the soul as it journeys towards a higher state, in either human or demi-godlike form. While such fictions do not contribute to a strictly scientific discussion of 'whether' and 'when', they do bear on grossly human reactions which will strongly impact not the 'whether' and 'when', but the 'what'. The 'what' was not explicitly part of this task. It is important to consider the 'what' since a mutant's existence among prejudiced and rationalizing humans will cause a strong reaction.

A reaction could well eliminate the mutation before it can breed to successful quantities.

Note an additional unknown factor to bear in mind is whether, when a mutation occurs, it is in a single individual one time, or if its 'time has come' and it begins occurring throughout a population. There is no evidence for the latter so we shall assume the former: one-time random unprompted occurrences. See attached data file.

The nature of the current homo sapiens race is viewed in my own analysis as being a potentially overwhelming negative factor for a new otherwise-successful mutation. Such an important factor even if the same mutation did occur repeatedly in a population or widely separate geographical areas, failure of the mutation is likely. Given the current variations among homo sapiens, it is not felt by this researcher such an occurrence tomorrow would have any chance whatsoever of procreating. The allowable constraints placed on defined 'normal' and physically ('esthetically') acceptable local norms limit change in such a way even modest alterations due to 'natural selection' breeding are severely curtailed. A true genetic mutant, of any conceivable significant type, would certainly be destroyed by current Homo Sapiens as odd or dangerous.

CONCLUSIONS:

There is agreement among Western and Asian communities that evolution among homo sapiens due to natural selection is continuing.

ATTACHMENT 158.1.1 As evidence, consider the variety of human physical forms and mental capabilities found throughout...

ATTACHMENT 158.1.2 As evidence of rejection outside narrow local norms, consider the record of...

158.2 There is agreement among Western and Asian communities on an average previous rate of occurrence of successful mutation of 2.8 million years. There is no agreement as to a next occurrence date, or whether such an occurrence is guaranteed within the previously experienced variation (from 0.75 million to 6 million years).

ATTACHMENT 158.2 As evidence, consider the archeological findings and datings...

158.3 Current homo sapiens will genocidally deal with individuals or even small communities of the next potentially superior mutation. While homo sapiens are the dominant life form and ignoring a severe alteration by genetic engineering, there will be no next successful mutation of the species of man.

ATTACHMENT 158.4 As evidence of the difference between previous successful species and homo sapiens in their ability to commit mutant genocide, consider the actions of newly Christianized Spain, after the expulsion of the Moors, against Jews perceived to be prospering better and possessing superior intelligence...etc.

In conclusion, it appears irrelevant as to whether the next advanced mutation will occur in a day, a hundred years, or another 2.8 million. The current dominant life form on this planet is of a technological type that has never before existed. One whose nature will prevent further natural mutations from breeding at any cost, and with religious fervor. Continued changes due to natural selection are anticipated but limited to a degree not heretofore likely in non-technological species. Natural breeding variations will be tempered by and compete with changes in man caused by man himself via genetic engineering. The results of the competition are beyond the scope of this task.

END TASK

5

Philanthropy

Reading the evening paper, he knew what he could do now. While the Athenas could measure the value of traditional corporate PR, and then task it as such, he doubted they had an appreciation for lynch mob mentality. Of just how fast anyone prospering during generally hard times could find themselves subject to an illogically hostile human response. Witch hunts. Cross burnings. House torchings. People gladly did this to other people without much prompting. And in this poverty ridden valley of Appalachia, it wouldn't take much to turn a neutral population hostile to 'those devil machines'. And they would stay hostile for a generation or more. The good news was, that the same human illogic would make local supporters fiercely loyal to each other in times of trouble, once you were thought of as one of the home team. This he knew, even if the Athenas didn't.

Eric Lorenz drove his Yamaha motorcycle out to where the rally for the President had passed. Now was the time to gauge local reaction. All Presidential security had disappeared, and few TV crews remained. Soon newspaper reporters and a single camera crew from Knoxville were left. It was then he turned to the burly Irishman standing at his left and said "Now." Eric himself walked straight ahead to the local reporters. These had gathered in a bunch, as much to decide on which bar to hit debriefing each other from the morning's events.

It wasn't much of a center of town, as out-of-towners quickly found. A single statue of some forgotten historic figure, surrounded by a well-manicured 20 ft square of stone and wood. About the square were parking spaces for about a dozen vehicles. Three roads led away from the square out of town, with stores lining both sides of each for no more than a few dozen yards. The local post office was the other source of statuary, though small, and included the obligatory flag pole and merrily waving flag.

The Presidential visit to Appalachia in this pre-election summer had national coverage written all over it. Announced as a new Presidential initiative to bring prosperity to the Appalachians. To those who missed the great surging US economy. The Governor and a senator from Kentucky were there. It was a national spotlight for local politicos. It was a national spotlight on the incumbent team they hoped would boost the VP's chances in the next presidential election. It was the kind of national spotlight the ARF would not want focused on them at present. Lorenz knew this and timed his approach. A word to the tired but pleasant group of reporters was all it took, and they were walking off to a nearby store porch where Eric's Irishman was gathering a crowd. With a booming voice of someone used to command, he drew in ten or twenty men and couples. Eric made sure the Knoxville TV crew saw the crowd and local reporters as a quick chance to wrap up the local reaction.

But what they all heard didn't sound like a political speech. What they heard was a simple man's call to arms to fix the roof of Alma Warren's shack. Alma was the local housekeeper lady, who barely kept an all-too-leaky roof overhead for herself and her Alzheimer stricken sister. Both in their 80s, they were profiled in the town paper Lorenz read two nights ago as local icons. As examples of how this administration's great plans would probably pass right by Alma and her sister. It was a heartfelt piece of writing.

Now Lorenz positioned himself within the crowd on the dusty street, listening to the ex-foreman of a now-closed brewery ask for men to come with him to put a new roof on the shack. When asked where the materials would come from — since everyone knew Alma hadn't a spare nickel — the Irishman said "That computer fellah's boss is buyin," pointing at Lorenz. When asked if it was a paying job, the Irishman stared the questioner straight in the eye and said, "Not a dime. I haven't worked for pay in a month either Bobby. But him and me can't do it alone. All I need is two good men to make fast work of it." Someone from the crowd (and Lorenz could have kissed her for asking), called out "What computer people?" The Irishman looked over to Lorenz and said "There's one now; Eric if you don't already know him. The crowd and reporters turned to face Eric, who stood his ground, hands in pockets. In the crowd. Among them. And spoke among them, but looked up at the big Irishman the whole time.

"I'm with Athena Robotics, up on Anderson Lane." He left out the foundation part. "We're in computers. My boss said he heard that same speech (gesturing to a now empty podium) from President Johnson 40 years ago, and nobody he knew personally ever got a cent of help out of it then either. He said our company will foot the bill for a new roof for Alma. Anybody who's seen it knows she's getting wet in the summer, snow in the winter, and pneumonia in between." There were knowing nods in the small crowd, even among the reporters. "He knows it's not much, but it's what we can afford to do. Oh, and he said any man who can afford some spare time to help gets to keep the hammers, saws, or whatever else we have leftover. God knows it's little enough."

As he looked up at the Irishman, with his voice lowered quietly during the last sentence, there was a pause followed by five men crowding up to the Irishman with 'count me ins' and 'I'm laid off anyway'.

The reporters, meanwhile, scribbled away furiously at what they saw as the cap to editorials of the day. More empty words from Washington, while neighbors helped neighbors. Lorenz brushed off their inquiries with 'that's Athena Robotics. No, no interviews. You guys have had enough politicians here today for that. We're just tryin' to make somethin' actually happen." and quickly strode away.

Two days later, Alma had a new roof on her 30ft x 15ft irregular shanty. Seven men divided up a stack of hammers, screwdrivers, and leftover nails and wood scrap. The tools were bought at the local hardware store. Tar paper and nails from the same. The 4' x 8' sheets of 1/2" plywood were bought at the local mill outlet in town. And the shingles ended up donated by that same mill. They had a stack laying around from tearing down an old building last fall. The ensuing editorials made Athena Robotics a new local hero. And mention of the event on the Knoxville local news — without mentioning the foundation or the mill by name — ticked off the locals who were proud to say "That was the Jameson Mill and those Athena computer people over on Anderson Lane that made it happen. And Knoxville wouldn't even mention them by name. Sons a bitches! Don't give us the time of day in Knoxville." By the time Friday had come and gone, and all the presidential gossip was traded at the local stores and shops, not a person within 35 miles of Valley didn't know Athena was one of ours. Cost to the firm: $647.43. Lorenz submitted the receipts.

***

"These people have been holding off tax revenuers and famine together for a century. I don't know if or when it'll be needed, but if something bad's coming up the road I'll bet we'll get at least one or two calls of warning. And whoever comes will be getting one or two bad directions down these muddy Tennessee dirt roads."

Lorenz was being debriefed by a trio of Athena Personnel, Athena Prime, and another human image on video he hadn't seen before. How did he know what to say to the other humans? And what would be effective? And why make up the 'boss' figure with the out of work foreman?

"I just spent that morning walking around and listening to what people in the crowd were saying. The locals, not the state politicians out for a photo opportunity. There was a lot of mixed apathy and anger out there. As for 'my boss', well, the 'President Johnson visit' line I got from an old woman at the market first thing that morning. She seemed to get a good reaction from saying it to her friends, so I just went with it. Kept the focus off me that way too.

The foreman is Tom Murphy. I met him at the dog kennel through Dr. Rearden. He was willing, but doubtful we'd get anyone. Maybe just one. But even he was gung ho by the time the volunteers started coming forward. Oh, DEFINE: Gung Ho = Enthusiastic. Actually, the hardest part was letting him do all the talking and organizing. I became just one of the hands. One of them."

***

TASK 108 WEBSITE REPORT

ASSIGNED: 06/26/20xx

COMPLETED: 08/01/20xx

LEAD AGENT: E. Lorenz ISSUING AGENT: A. Personnel

TASK DEFINITION:

Part 108.1 Content of an ARF website. Specify data we should acknowledge publicly, data to specifically withhold, and contact data for the ARF and other robotic sites.

Part 108.2 Technical requirements and funding for an ARF website.

Part 108.3 Conclusions as related to ARF project security.

REFERENCES: Non-ARF Files

SCHEDULE: Two calendar months from inception

RESULT:

A website similar to other non-profit scientific organizations. Setup like a group whose primary purpose is the collection and dissemination of information on the robotics industry by supporting High School contests and robot clubs. All collected data from other organizations should be collated and referenced. Have links to other good robotics websites, including government projects like NASA Robotics and university sites like MIT AI Lab and Cambridge and the Princeton efforts. Have a favorite robot design of the week. Have free downloads of papers and schematics.

Setup a secondary page for robotic competitions and students. Include lessons in robots 101, home hobby construction projects, basic principles, lots of photos, and links to the FIRST Robotics and Battlebots competitions. Solicit donations which will be used to support local robot clubs and high school programs.

Technically, a plain multi-page site from CompUWeb or a similar vendor will work well. Large data storage is not required, but several downloadable files (data, schematics, etc) must be on the server at additional cost. Links to other sites and a contact list with email comes with hosted pages. See attached cost breakdown.

As a federal non-profit organization, funds can be legally solicited onsite. Do so on the homepage and with a link to a more detailed page on the uses of funds (support this website, high school programs, etc.) and how to donate. Donations can be made using PayPal and Verisign with an Amex/Visa/MC merchant account (ignore Discover and other lesser cards). Donations in set amounts of $10 $25 $100 and $other.

As a non-profit foundation, we should sign up with several search engines under 'foundations' and register as a philanthropy where appropriate to drive further donations. There are modest registration fees. See attached.

As a further source of funds for the project, not shown on the primary website, will be an audiotex (automated telephone) sex service for adult males. This is profitable and was previously performed by researcher Jean Hunley for a client in Manhattan. That service used a combination of recorded and live females; we will be focusing on recorded to eliminate the need for human staff. If approved, a business plan will be developed and implemented on a separate web address. Jean's files include 350 hours of 'stories' from a dozen girls.

The main site can be a central clearing point for each satellite office using a secured intranet page. This will allow those with appropriate usernames, passwords, and fixed known IP addresses to get in. Landline telephones and cell phones are completely insecure; email can be made secure against all but Echelon-type governmental eavesdropping.

We should keep abreast of hacking, cracking, and spyware techniques for defensive purposes. All websites and blog sites dealing with finance (i.e. donations) are subject to attack. A human on staff with those skills, such as J. Hunley, is recommended as this is something beyond current Athena skills.

The internal intranet site should be a separate domain name and IP address from Network Associates or their successor agencies. Block from search engine (Google/Yahoo/MSN/Lycos) access. Remove blocks after bugs are corrected. Even then, no critical internal data should be posted. Critical data may be passed but in a transitory manner. Machines on which critical data is stored will not be connected to the internet. Data will be checked and transferred via a third set of machines used for transfer. On the transfer platforms, full viral, worm, and spyware scanning will be performed.

END TASK

6

Coincidence

Late in the afternoon, he sat alone, as usual, in the small room passing as a cafeteria. A single microwave oven humming, an old fashioned toaster over with a coffee maker by its side, both working hard and a nice little bar fridge for his milk. His thoughts ran to the latest upgrade he noticed in the Athenas. From his first day with them, they exhibited head movement and facial emotional expressions which he later confirmed were generated by the Houston head system of VERA. It was equipped to locate and track human faces during a conversation. In addition, the first generations of VERA returned whatever facial expression was seen in the nearest human by a series of 27 relays tugging on the face. A complex, but somewhat unsatisfying start. The Athenas he saw today, though, were uniformly different than yesterday. Even the dogs seemed to notice their direct stares and noticing specific objects at random. On questioning, they referred him to an upgrade they received from someone at the Computer Science Dept at Stamford in gaze-corrected videoconferencing techniques coupled with new real-time video image mapping. The improved polygon rendering from the human at another office like this one and chroma-keying techniques from a task winner at the Southwest Research Institute in Texas were startling. They had managed to layer the improved imaging onto the controls feed for facial movements from VERA. Lorenz likened it to the way the mammalian brain overlays commands onto an essentially reptilian core in primates. He thought there was more to the layering technique that had yet to be explored and spent several pleasant hours in reverie; letting his mind jump from idea to idea, allowing the concepts to wash over him without concern for a specific problem or solution. The gift of lateral thinking was made enjoyable here, instead of past jobs where such 'daydreaming' was shunned or outright laughed at. Most humans would never know the pure joy of creative thought, not because they were incapable, but because where they were physically or in their life would not lend itself to such selfish and seemingly non-productive self-indulgence.

As the evening progressed, the sounds of crickets and night noises outside his office window began to pleasantly distract him. Three months into the job, the daily lullaby was soft and comforting. It matched the rightness of the code he wrote for the data-mining queries in SQL Access, the truth of an automated feedback system he knew would work. The beauty of the mathematics he had worked out. His mind drifted in harmony with the sounds, and before he was conscious of it, consciousness had left him peacefully asleep at his desk.

The light from his window awakened him. 'My Gods, its morning already!' he though almost aloud. Stiff in his movement to sit up straight, Lorenz could feel the creases must be on his face from where it lay half the night on the collection of documents, sketches, and paraphernalia on his desk. Lorenz stretched and stood, moving out to the uncluttered center of the small room, and did a few squats, followed by pushups. The thoughts and sureness of the night before flooded back to him as he breathed in deeply with each push. He lay on the floor for a few more moments thinking through his conclusions and some of the details as well. He smiled in a way he hadn't since his first job out of college. A note of hunger made itself known as he rolled to his bare feet and padded out the door, seeking the machine he knew was waiting like a patient servant to serve him, even early on a Saturday morning. Bear claws and coffee. The analogy to an Athena serving a man began to assert itself as his still sleepy mind streamed thoughts slowly but with gathering momentum. All half thoughts were abruptly cut off when he heard a man's voice coming from Athena Prime's office. A human male. The voice of a stranger.

In this secure facility, whose security measures he suspected he hadn't even noticed the half of, his caution was aroused. With stealth, he approached the open door to her office and stood by listening.

"Refresh queries on human historical assumptions. Range equal between [–750] years and [+100] years. Best guess Simpson technique."

'Summary or detail, Founder,' said the voice of Athena Prime. Founder? He listened more intently.

"Summary. Highlight changes made since last verbal summary please." The man's voice was distant, as though distracted by other thoughts, yet precise in tone and cadence. The founder?

'New data and conclusions: Primary features of Terran society at –750 years best characterized in European dark ages, parallel to eastern Asian Confucianism/Shintoism and North American low-tech harmonic balance with nature. Human Talents are generally suppressed in a grim struggle for existence. Reading and writing limited to cleric class. Political leaders and laborers illiterate. Scientific advancement stifled. Inventions stolen from Talents as soon as revealed, thereby providing no incentive for additional Talent innovations and progress. Thought processes suppressed by reliance on superstitious beliefs explaining multiple unknowns. Crowd control primary tool is ignorance. The methods included religious stories...

"Stop please," interrupted the man, "Scroll ahead to late nineteenth-century Europe."

'Building on the physical and intellectual tools created by Talents of the Italian renaissance, individual Talent families of combined ambition and ability amassed great fortunes and power, built corporate and political empires, and controlled economies and governments. Individuals each continued the logical advancement of the Industrial Revolution in specific limited fields, the whole of which relied on each cross-field advancement for the next leap in a non-related field. The selfishness philosophy of Ayn Rand was followed without conscious forethought, as a natural method. Philanthropy level was minimal compared to incidental assistance to the masses by the great works themselves. Grants for schools, libraries, museums, and basic research projects received most of the concentrated wealth that was consciously distributed. Inheritance of the rest of concentrated wealth generally squandered on leisure and physical pleasures within two generations by descendants. '

"Stop. Scroll ahead to current decade please."

'Clinton-Gore American example the primary economic engine of the world. Other societies use older failing models. Direct result of misdirection of Reagan responsibility-of-self and economic success in previous decade. Alzheimer's drug successfully implemented by opponents. Tarnishing of potential Talent heroes by drug, violence, and sex scandals. Best successes with sports figures and entertainers. Work ethic out of favor. Engineering of Milliken imprisonment tarnished first Wall Street generally, then anyone with overt financial success in the eyes of young adults. Accepted by Politicians as justification for their own scandals. Feedback in media results in desensitization of the masses. Clinton presidency seen as model for 'humanitarian' person: advocacy of community thought and consensus over individual heroism; individual priorities on 'do anything to get re-elected', indulgence in illicit sensual pleasures, betrayal of oaths of office, and marriage ignored by electorate. Gore presidency seen as model for 'righteous' person: misdirection, 'government knows better than private industry', people must be protected against themselves, suppression of news of breakthroughs such as cloning of the rich and powerful.'

'In recent years, the public distracted by fascist division and the rise of violent political factions...'

"Stop. That's America. Detail confirmatory evidence for analysis on international level please."

'Specific detail to Clinton false humanitarian model: NATO attacks Serbian Yugoslavia, humanitarian relief of Kosovo kills more Kosovars in bombing than Serbian army. NATO earlier ignored larger-scale wars in Chechnya (100,000 dead), Bosnia (35,000 dead), Sierra Leone (225,000 dead). UN ignored Cambodia (3.8 million dead) for 20 years while grieving over a few dozen Palestinians. Ignored areas were under governments with distributed leadership and no oil. Serbian Dictator seen as individual of strength and ability. Discredited individual leadership by labeling him a war criminal. Trump withdrew troops from Syria, allowing the Russian slaughter of freedom rebels, then his troop withdrawal from Germany encouraged Putin to invade Ukraine. Other examples.'

"Continue summary. Scroll to projection for year 2025 please."

'Educational changes over 20 years result in acknowledgment that individuals who are not risk takers but work by consensus now run Fortune 1000 corporations. Talents who display both ambition and ability are publicly discredited ala-Milliken model. Branded unfair. Non-work focuses on pleasures for both workers and management judged the norm. Politicians who are perceived 'humanitarian' ala Clinton model win marginally more elections than 'righteous' Gore-type politicians. Free-thinking Rand/Reagan models publicly vilified. Environmental problems in developed nations minimized locally, resulting in apathy among the masses and leaders alike. Environmental problems globally increasing geometrically as third world countries given knowledge of early industrial revolution power and transport techniques via 'humanitarian aid'. Water supply in industrialized nations approaching critical levels of pollutants. Ozone layer sufficiently damaged to drive leisure in tech countries indoors (no tanning) in solitary (no human opponent) VR games. Wars become local to regional, as large distant enemies become difficult to pinpoint. Terrorism and personal revenge methods rise, feeding anti-individual action opinions of the masses. Third-world nations war openly. Human population at 7 billion. Athenas common in tech countries as wheelchair office models in 2011. Assistants. Danger recon scouts. Arial attack drones. Pleasure droids on black market. VR enhancers. Evolution of personal computing devices keeps demand for more staff who are fluent in 1 or 2 or 3 computer language generations high, even after newer models released.'

'End of Summary. Is there anything else, Founder?'

The unseen man paused at this point. Not much had changed. His voice cracked with age. "Continue summary mode. Scroll ahead to projection of computer design plateau year please."

'Core common language reached in voice to code translator 2035. Thereafter, coding irrelevant to humans, only results. Programming per se is no longer required. This results in drop of the heretofore large need for the best minds to enter the computing field. Mechanics and technicians only. Pay drops. The last place where high levels of educational training required is gutted. AI systems are everything except the hands needed to wield actions, as exemplified by engineers, corporate leaders, attorneys, and politicians. Doctors lead though diagnoses and robotic operations. Engineers encounter cost/benefit projections limiting new innovations. Corporate and financial leaders rely increasingly on statistical analyses to provide probabilities of profitable courses of action. Politicians continue reliance on polls and spin techniques.

Resulting widespread influence of human decisions by AI systems. Control of scattered AI systems has potential to provide control over humans though subtle data manipulation. Most human jobs are for 'craft' labor and middle management.'

'Raw scientific knowledge reaches accumulated level of volume and complexity where no single human can gestalt enough information to make the next innovative leap. Team failures at critical data overflow point within 3 more years. Only the Athenas can still cross-discipline enough to invent. Athenas keep putting the pieces together to form a whole picture and see individual discipline and sub-discipline works assigned to brilliant Talents. The Talents themselves will be well rewarded, sated with pleasures, but have no real idea of how their work fits into the whole. The 1960s feeling they are a cog in the wheel returns and will be encouraged. Human population controlled to fall to 4 billion in 50 years and dropping using infertility weapons in tech nation's water supply, confirming the false human premise from the 1970s technological cultures "naturally" have lower birth rates. Accepted by self-indulgent masses and Talents alike. Third-world nations lead to agricultural/mining economies, thereby dropping the need for more electrical power and reducing worldwide environmental impact. Lower local population decreases need for intensive fertilizers to feed current population levels. Human-on-human genocidal wars and euthanasia assist in the effort. African populations decimated by AIDS, then TRG; re-populated by European Moslems and Arabs. Global cooling returns to a level humans notice; Talents are the first. False global warming hoax revealed, attributed to mistake of individual scientists of the 1990s and early 2000s. Cooling cuts agricultural production which is insufficiently supported by high-energy technologies. Population falling seen as a good thing by most humans.'

"Stop. Date of alarm of human leaders as to falling population levels please."

'Outside scope of projection ability maintaining at least 30% probability. Beyond year 2100. Eventual perception by humans, if ever, deemed irrelevant.'

Lorenz found himself not breathing towards the end of this part of the briefing. What was he listening to? Surely this was not an attempt to predict the course of human actions and events like Asimov? Or even more frightening, were these aspects of an actual plan being carried out today, in place since at least the Reagan years, and looking forward for the next hundred? An Alzheimer drug? Framing Milliken? Discrediting men like Gates & Musk?

Then he heard an odd sound from the man inside the doorway, not 10 feet away. It was a sigh. The kind someone makes when disappointed something else was not found out. A tone of voice indicating nothing new was revealed. Or perhaps an additional desired projection was not yet deemed probable. The man continued in a different vein.

"Current projected date of bi-pedal Athenas in open human society, please."

'Bipedal motion planned introduction publicly in year 2027, Founder'

The sign again. "And the estimated likelihood of human anti-robot sentiment if introduction of bipedal Athenas in original earlier proposal?"

Athena was silent for a moment, thinking the problem through. Thinking, thought a frightened Lorenz. No, he told himself. It's just running a series of complex joins and data-mining queries. She's not thinking.

'If bi-pedal Athenas displayed before 2011, 85% likely widespread backlash. 93% likely violent. 63% likely incorporation into a Luddite religious movement. Warning: this alteration in plan not recommended in the strongest of terms.'

"Yes, yes. Correct. But soon unavoidable. Continue plan with milestones unedited. Thank you, Athena."

'I appreciate your input, Founder. May I suggest we have these talks more often, and in detail mode on specific milestones?'

"Unavoidably not possible at present. As soon as working Athenas provide sufficient income to the Foundation, I will shift my priorities to advising you on plan details. For now, it's up to you, dear. And you're doing fine."

'Thank you for your confidence, Founder. I look forward to seeing you again soon.'

With that, Lorenz broke out of his frozen surveillance and rapidly backed down the hall to his own office again. Ducking inside as the man Athena referred to as Founder emerged from her office, lost in his own thoughts. His path was straight out of the building, which thankfully for Lorenz did not bring him past his open office door. With security what it was, the visitor never gave a thought to someone else being in the building. The mistake the stranger made on entering the building was asking Athena Reception if any staff arrived or left today. She responded pleasantly no one had, which was true. For today began at midnight.

Thus Lorenz was unaccounted for in the strange visitor's mind, leaving him in a position to know what no other human alive might know. For the first time in 100,000 years, something other than primates was competing for the title of dominant life form on this planet. Lorenz stayed in his office for the next few hours, thinking. Unaccountably, the more he thought, the less frightened he became. Realizing this, he could not determine if the abatement of his fear was due to its natural replacement by rational thought. Or if the nature of what he heard was itself less frightening as he began to see its implications. For humans. For himself.

***

People suck. Just look how we treat each other and our own children half the time."

Doc Rearden looked a little sideways at Lorenz and shook his head in the negative.

"You looking for someone to agree with you, son?"

They both sat for a moment as Lorenz let his thoughts focus on what he felt. How had people made the world better? How had they made his own life what it was? No matter what he did or tried, it seemed the bulk of humanity was against him. Was playing him. Was using him. His thoughts took him to the dark place he seldom spoke of out loud.

"I'll die without children, Doc. Maybe for the better." There. He said it. Now Doc would tell him what everyone else had. He was still young. So his first 2 marriages ended badly. So he was lied to about abortions, about hysterectomies, as the women he loved knew how to play him. Knew his jelly spot.

Doc shook his head again, "I'm not with you there. Sometimes just getting laid can clear a guy's head if it's been a while. Has it been a while, Eric?"

Lorenz was a bit startled at this turn in the conversation. "Getting laid has never been a problem. It's my choices that are bad."

"So you're a schmuck with girls, and they know it. You're an accident looking to happen. So just don't go that far. Just have a good time for a while." His gaze took in the waitress approaching and Lorenz's gaze joined his. Doc noticed once again how Lorenz was intent on her movements, and how she knew it. But Eric always looked away when it became obvious she would notice him noticing. Doc shook his head, this time with a smile, and said out loud, "Lisa, sweetie, this fine young man would like to make your acquaintance but wanted me to do the formal introduction bit. Ha."

Lorenz looked up from the swirling bubbles in his beer in surprise, glanced at Lisa, then back at Doc with incredulity, dropping his tensed shoulders. Lisa smiled at both of them and laughed an easy laugh, knowing Eric had said no such thing.

"What's he got, no tongue?" Then seeing Eric was now beyond the ability to form coherent sentences with her this close to him, she moved closer still. Eric swore he could feel the warmth of her skin, the heat coming off her palpable. Doc and the rest of the room faded away as he was taken in by her hand on his shoulder.

"Don't let Doc bother you, doll. He's just jealous you're younger and cuter than he is." So many responses swept thru Eric's mind he said three of them at once. Lisa laughingly gave his shoulder a final squeeze as she withdrew from him. A lingering touch left him with a visible communication of how he felt by the alteration in his jeans. The hand was gone but she had not moved an inch away. The scent of her was so strong.

"I'm Eric since the Doc isn't going to help me out — with actually telling you." He tried to sound light and cool, but as usual, revealed how intently she had affected him.

"I'm Lisa," she responded, and they continued in what passed for flirtatious banter. Eric began to grow more confident as he told her in 25 seconds where he worked, where he was from, and before he knew it, had asked her out to the local movie. Somehow.

And somehow her number appeared as if by magic on a napkin. "See you tomorrow in front of the movie at 8." And off she trotted, another conquest in hand.

Eric's smile was plastered on his face as he and Doc drank a toast together to women everywhere, the givers of pain and delight. "Just be careful with this one, son. Just fun, right?"

Eric agreed wholeheartedly, "Sure, sure, just a movie, just a little more if I get lucky."

Doc grunted "Oh that's not even in question. She already likes you well enough for that. And you're new meat. And educated. Not her usual fare. Just remember not to make stupid promises or lose yourself just 'cause you're getting some."

Eric was too happy to take the Doc's comments any way but in his best interests, as they were intended. They toasted again, draining their mugs, and ordered one more round.

***

Their conversation was observed by a discrete shadow in the far corner of the bar. Too far to overhear, but much could be and was gleaned by an astute observer. Another waitress stopped briefly by his table, but the old man sitting in the shadow waved her off with an economy of movement. He continued to sip his beer, something he seldom drank. The chicken wings he ordered were long since cold. To order something more to his taste, like a little Chambord or a sweet port, would have drawn unwanted attention. Beer and wings wouldn't raise an eyebrow in this or any part of suburban Tennessee. From his seat, he watches for the result he had hoped for and dreaded. He knew what he now must do. Focus of the young man must be maintained. A female entanglement now would be ill-timed. And if he was found out, anger against what the old man had in mind was far more useful an emotion than the despair of Lorenz's too recently disintegrated marriage.

After Doc Rearden and Lorenz left together, the old man in the corner paid his bill in cash and slipped out into the dark of the evening. Coughing and pulling his coat tighter around his neck against the cool night air, the gray-haired octogenarian moved with pain known best to the aged. Seldom enough to stop what you were doing, but enough to be a constant reminder of how few days were ahead, and how many had long since passed you by. As he walked to the back of the gravel and dirt parking lot and neared his old Volvo, he paused at a sight he always expected and never looked forward to. A looming figure waiting with practiced patience. Unobtrusive. Generic at a distance. Forgettable.

"I'm still working. I'm still alive." One of the advantages of his age was not to mind stating the obvious. He needed to say something first to maintain his courage. The quiet figure waited for the old man to approach a few feet closer.

"We were concerned about the opening of so many facilities. In so many locations," said the Other.

"Five is not so many," responded the gray man, shivering slightly in the cool air. "They're temporary. And the approach was to be left completely to me without interference. Has this changed?"

"This has not changed. We will not interfere. Rather, I am here to inform you of the procedure at the end. We anticipate either you or the work is close to point of … Observation." The old man shook again, but this time not with the cold. "Come and we will speak further where it is warmer." The two figures, cloaked in the darkness, drifted off into the night.

7

Recruits

Gracie Koziol sat in her parent's kitchen. This was the place where family talks always happened. This is where they fed her what she now knew to be patronizing compliments her whole life. They were again feeding her what they thought she needed to hear to get her out on her own. As a sociology student, she excelled in her intuitive understanding of complex relationships in a way her family could never understand. Their eyes glazed over each time she tried to talk about what she had hoped would become her life's work. But after steering her to a disastrous internship with 'special' youths, they now revealed all she should expect, all there would be for her — what else was she going to do with a sociology degree except coddle some low life into getting their paperwork thru the government services programs available to them? Who did she think she was? Young, slim, and sweet-natured, she could have focused on the pre-med boys at school instead of grades but no, don't listen to us your own family. Family response to questions on her chosen path in research tonight at that well-worn kitchen table let her know they didn't care. Marking time until you marry. Nothing you do is important. The comments she received from one of her professor's acquaintances said otherwise. He had read a paper she submitted on human religious responses to new technology. When they met, he told her he thought it was special — that she was special.

Mike Serruzi was a wiz at engines. All kinds. Since he started telling his stepfather and older brothers how to better tune their cars. Since he revealed to his classmates how inept and rote thinkers their professors on power systems were. They had barely passed him with a D in new power concepts when he submitted a paper on how to power robots with sucrose/cellulose engines, so machines could feed and get their power organically. His professors at NYU and friends alike met his ideas with sneers and derision. He was surprised when he saw an online article on how Melhuish and his team at the University of the West of England in Bristol developed a robot to catch flies and digest them in a reactor cell generating electricity from the chitin sugar in their exoskeletons. Gastrobots. By the time Mike graduated from NYU with mediocre grades, he was unsurprised to find himself having little interest in serving someone else's needs for a paycheck. And with those lackluster grades was not offered anything interesting in the power field. He initially took a clerical job at the local IRS office; boring but it paid his bills. The thing giving him a little spark was a Battlebots contest he found on cable TV, and then that weird, short kid who kept pumping him for robotic power solutions. An email from the kid's 'grandfather' was even weirder, but he would go check it out anyway. What else was he doing with himself?

Steve Hoffman — electronics, circuitry, magnetic door locks for his high school pot stash. The skinny nerd everyone pictures at the word 'geek'. Pissing his life away designing toys for kids no one would ever buy, according to his family: old-world European craftsmen all. He was a disappointment. They laughed when the copyright he filed for a flying insect exterminator based on some of Tesla's work was rejected as "not believed feasible". He spent a night in the attic, tearfully re-reading the rejection notice while standing in front of his working device. Each time a spark took out another moth or mosquito, he vowed to never again let anyone tell him he couldn't make his 'stupid ideas' work. By morning he would be packed and gone. He'd make his own way in the world.

Thomas J Nestor liked the tone of the emails from the eccentric who wanted some help on old programming languages. No one wanted to know SHRDLU, LISP, or CPM variants anymore. All the money in America was being made by young kids in Java and modifying Microsoft kernels or SQL network command structures. He was too old, they said. Ukrainian by birth, an ex-physics high school teacher. But was the work he could get after emigrating. An ex-Soviet scientist who didn't want to work in their weapons programs. Knew lots of older computer languages nobody seemed to even remember. A man without a mission. Until that eccentric called.

***

An old man sits alone in the dark. Bright light hurts his vision; steals with distraction what little time he has left in his cataract-infested left eye. Eventually, he thinks, we will need a common facility. One place to pool our efforts. A secure facility where we can work together, uninterrupted, and unobserved. It would have to be quite private. Off the grid. Relatively self-sustaining, since the more contact we have with any surrounding community the larger the chance of discovery. It's one thing to have a little place or office of your own and blend in unobtrusively. But when the dozen or so talents are assembled, well, they would be an odd crowd even in a sophisticated metropolitan area. They would stand out as a clique in a university environment.

We need a private place. I'll sell the St. Louis rental property at a profit. Mortgage rates are down, prices up. Everything else was temporary anyway.

Stay away from the coastlines. An anti-technology group helping Greenpeace with nailing and spiking trees to prevent the lumberjacks from cutting them, they've graduated to wrecking tech offices near Seattle and burning developments in woodlands on Long Island. Best to keep a low profile and out of those areas.

I should start with the old place in Montana. Remote. Elevated away from the shorelines. The highest security problem may be the world-wide war on terrorism. It used to be only ranchers, retirees, and survival nuts lived there. Now, with border crossing concerns via Canada as well as the more publicized Mexican problems, the government is sure to have agents throughout the high country monitoring obvious collections of people who just did not belong, to root out terrorist cells. Like the one they found in Buffalo NY. That one was fronted by a fake jewelry shop. We'll have to be careful. The talents were not selected for this skill set, so I'll have to make the preparations myself. Ready or not, when the work reaches its critical phase, I'll bring them all in here. And from here we shall succeed or fail.

***

Athena2 made her usual understated appearance at Lorenz's door. 'Hello, Mr. Lorenz. Am I disturbing you?'

"Come in. I'm downloading something. I'll be done in a minute."

'Please come to my office when you are free.' And with that, she was gone.

"Ok," he called after her, noting again how relaxed his language was becoming around the Athenas. With no apparent loss in clarity. Then he stopped what he was doing for a moment. She had always waited patiently before, or went away and came back. This was the first time she opted for the logically more complex 'see me when you're done'. Was this growth by experience or were the Athenas advancing again?

He couldn't tell. Perhaps a new language module or upgrade. But from who or where?

Fifteen minutes later, he was seated in Athena2's office. He had entered using the same attention (I'm here) short query (Free?) and if-then action set the Athenas were using. It had become a habit with him. It was an easy logical approach that he knew they understood. And it was polite. Human-to-human speech syntax was far more difficult. And unclear.

Athena 2 presented him with a new task. This one would be ongoing until terminated. Apparently, the SONY electronics corporation of Japan has been active in Robotics research for many years, since the early 1980s. Several interesting firsts were attributed to their labs, including a 7ft tall walking bi-pedal robot P2 (1994) and an advanced vision system P3 (1997). One of their continuing projects was the introduction of robots into Japanese households. In Japan, such a venture had a willing and excited techno market with little or no fear of robots whatsoever. Lacking was the availability of product. SONY had hit on what it thought was a pretty good entry point: a robotic dog. The 1998 model was a significant advance over previous betas and was put into production. For $2500 US, RoboPet comes with camera eyes, microphone, touch screens, and 18 motors mimicking the motion of a dog in how it walks, sits, and lies down. The next generation RoboPet was advertised as responsive to simple voice commands, like roll over and come. It will also provide an audio/video link when you're away from home, so you can monitor the kids or the housekeeper.

The ARF, it turned out, owned every one of the betas leading to this version, and those of competitors, and now one of these as well. The premise was not to keep abreast of the state of the art. By acting as paying customers, the ARF provided user feedback to the manufacturers. In such a small consumer group, their voice was heard and their influence felt. This new RoboPet, however, had a potential sales volume large enough to make one consumer's voice a lot smaller than it now was. For this reason, Lorenz was to keep track of the progress of robotic pets.

All vendors, not only Sony. Hardware and software changes. Feature changes. Sales volume and demographics. Planned innovations. The task intended to find a way to maintain at least some influence on the direction of these products. The success or failure of his efforts would, in the long run, influence foundation decisions on whether to even attempt such influence on future products from competing vendors, as well as other product lines within the leader, Sony. As it turned out, cheap imitations spread like wildfire into numerous homes over the next few Christmas seasons. Everything from Poochie to Radio Shack versions.

Unmentioned, and unasked by Lorenz, was why the ARF sought such influence. What were their long-term goals? For it did strike Lorenz they were asking him to play a vital role in what had to be a multi-year task. He felt like part of this foundation now, to be so assigned, and was determined to aggressively pursue the subject. Not knowing the full resources of the Foundation, or even how deep their pockets are, he would not limit his analysis in any way. He learned on previous tasks to ask, and if the answer was 'No we can't, or won't, or it exceeds our area budget', then fine. No stigma was surprisingly attached to him for asking. All they did ask was he keep those ideas coming, keep thinking. Lorenz knew before he left the room his approach would consider everything from putting a SONY employee on the payroll as a spy to an unlikely hostile takeover of SONY itself. As it turned out, he succeeded in far more modest, but important starting points in the first few months. A Foundation newsletter and website on the 'personal home' robotics industry — data which the foundation was already collecting in one form or another — and was published free to its first three 'complimentary' subscribers, all junior staff in the SONY robotics section in Japan and a few dozen more to key US universities. An extended free subscription was offered if they filled out a short questionnaire on where they thought the future of the robotics industry was heading. Eric's second real action was a purchase of 100 shares of SONY stock for the Foundation portfolio, whereby quarterly reports, updates, and names of key officers would all be made available to the Foundation. Attention: ARF Contact Franklin Wu.

***

Some days later, Lorenz was looking over a report on aesthetic design for systems. Ergonomics. Human factors for keyboards. The idea was to understand why certain systems were emotionally warm for users in a touchy-feely way not easily described without sounding like an art student. It struck Lorenz the lone great artist he knew who was also a scientist was DaVinci. His sculptures were classics and his portrait of the human form and its mathematical ratios was a poster found in every university dorm in America, right next to that year's Sports Illustrated swimsuit girls.

It occurred to him there were certain values, certain ratios in nature, such as DaVinci's use of the Fibonacci series and the Golden Section of 0.608 which kept recurring throughout nature. Rabbits, cows, Nautilus shell spirals, how leaves grow for maximum sunlight, bird triangles in flight for lift. He didn't know if there was a god or gods who were consciously reusing such values in all the designs of life. But the values were there. And the Golden Section was a key component. And he couldn't help feeling the Athenas would be more acceptable to humans if their proportions were slightly modified with these ratios in mind. He would be sure to recommend their next physical chassis upgrade adhere to proportioning.

Thinking of mathematical ratios concerning Athenas, he had a thought. He knew a lot of their parameters were hard coded. If this – then that. But the method failed with subjects you were trying to make appreciate the complex world in which we find ourselves. Throwing lines of code at the problem failed in the AI programs of the 1960s for that reason. As the millions of lines of code piled up, the systems became untenable. The neural net people in the 70s had their day too, and also failed. The drives for these Athenas were something in between, a combination of both approaches. Perhaps like the chess program at IBM had finally beaten the human World's champion. Easily. It had the unfortunate limitation of specialization. Already he had met an Athena Prime (the decision maker), and A. Reception, A. Personnel, and others over the web. But the part of the specialization troubling him today concerned a task report he read on reproductive methods. Combining code from two or more computer systems was common enough now, if still complex. Not in AI systems yet, but the report showed it's what someone had in mind for the ladies.

What bothered Lorenz was predictability. Variations on a theme. Something beyond the hard coding of DNA in human parents is what Darwin described in Descent of Man. Our children, in fact, the children of all mating life forms, were more than the strict clear combination of =their parents. More than 60%A + 40% B or A's blue eyes but B's height. Variations on a theme. Slight mutations, uncontrolled or unanticipated variations. If they proved viable, they continued to the next generation. If not, namely if the subject did not live long enough to reproduce, then the variation was not viable by definition.

For the Athenians, it was more than changing a few hard-coded settings. True variance was random but finite. Reasonable. A baby dog would not be born with gills instead of lungs. Or full-fledged wings. He thought a folded Möbius strip was a neat way to introduce such variations. Take a folded finite space. Better yet, a nonorientable surface is one of the three possible surfaces obtained by sewing a Möbius strip to the edge of a disk. The surface is a model of the projective plane without singularities and is a sextic surface. Map the fixed parameters of Athenas onto the outer surface. Create a secondary map of the distances between these points of data on the twisting curvature. This would be the variable. Not the data content of the points themselves, but the data resulting from changing the geometric parameters of the Möbius surface. Instead of one small change being one number, a single small change would alter the entire data map and hundreds of variables. But not the core design. He smiled and began searching the web for a Mathematica site showing numerous such constructs from Dietz to double boy toroids.

A sculpture of the surface he finally chose in Euclidean 3-space was installed at the library of the Mathematisches Forschungsinstitut Oberwolfach library building on January 28, 1991. Seeing the photo and trying to visualize which of the shapes was best suited to this type of effort was genuine fun.

8

Cause and Effect

Lorenz was useless this morning. Last night they had done it. The barmaid, Lisa Grushka, was all he hoped for after their night out at the movies. Nothing happened that night, a little kiss goodbye, but it was enough. He thought of little else when she invited him over on Saturday to have lunch at her house and meet her children. He ended up staying until Monday morning. And was useless at work this morning thinking of her.

After ten years of a decaying marriage, a woman like Lisa was a joy to behold. Energetic in bed to the point of draining Eric of all other thoughts. And when he couldn't anymore, she seemed quite happy with mutual oral pleasures, cuddling, and stroking each other. Until he could again. And again.

But that was at night when he and Lisa finished tucking in her children. Children who intently watched and observed them together. The days had belonged entirely to the three kids, 5, 10, and 15. The little girl Leah was the youngest, but by no means the most demanding. Lisa introduced Eric to them as a scientist and the boys were soon all over him. Jon at ten was eager and willing with every new idea around the house Lisa and Eric spoke of as she gave him the tour. This wall needed painting. This floor was torn out from water damage, but she hadn't had the money to replace it yet. A fatherless boy that age was overjoyed when Eric mentioned he would love to help and had done quite a bit of painting over the years. But not this first weekend. Now they were talking about their shared experiences of owning a home, fixing things up, and the simple pleasure of accomplishment those things gave. The fifteen-year old, Evan, was a bit quieter than the others at first but hung onto every word shared. He already saw Eric was the kind of man he could talk to. About guy things. And be talked to in turn, not talked at or yelled at. Not criticized for everything he said or did, like Lisa's last husband. Not abused verbally or otherwise for being so slow with most things. This man was different than his mom's usual fare. Strong but quiet.

The youngest, Leah, was the last to warm to Lorenz. Or so he thought. Throughout the first weekend, she would run up to him, showing him some toy or object, and then run away while Eric was still showing interest in it or explaining to her what it was for. Her attention seemed everywhere, but little known to this man with no children of his own, her attention was more finely tuned and focused on him than he could have imagined. With straight orange-blonde hair, she was otherwise her mother's twin, with a slightly rounder face, unstressed as yet by life.

At breakfast on Sunday, the children awoke to find Eric still there. The boys openly inquired where he had slept, the couch, or what. Eric let Lisa handle such inquiries in her gentle way and went about the task of making pancakes for the family. It would become their Sunday morning big breakfast together. The children were amazed he cooked. Sometimes burnt them a little. But how good a pancake was with raisins in it!

Over the next few weeks, Eric and Lisa spoke of many things. Of everything mattering to them both. Of family. Of wanting to get a set of phonics tapes to help Leah read and improve Jon's reading too. Of Evan's poor grades which threatened to drop him out of high school. One of Lisa's old boyfriends owned a garage in town and would take Evan on, but only after he got his diploma. Jon was academic in the family, with a sharp mind learning fast, whether it was Eric showing him how to saw wood, paint, or use a drill, or whether it was something new in school. The reports Lisa showed Eric from Jon's teachers all contained the common theme of underachievement. His mind was good, but his reading skills were poorly developed and it was hurting his grades. As they talked about how to work on all these things, Lorenz found himself being immersed in the family life he had always wanted. It was consuming.

And then there was Leah. It wasn't long before Eric had to be the last one to tuck her in at night, or she wouldn't stay down. It wasn't long before they fell into a fixed routine every evening after dinner of Leah on Eric's lap while Lisa cleared and cleaned. Leah had a selection of first-reader booklets and picture books of words, and every night they would sit together as he read and had her read whichever ones she chose. Often it was the same story or picture book, and he could see her vocabulary growing. Even Jon sat nearby now and then, waiting for his turn. But with Jon, it was sometimes reading, sometimes learning to play chess (which Lorenz loved), and sometimes sorting screws and bolts from a jar Jon had found one day in the basement. There didn't seem to be enough hours in the day for any of them. Eric's quality time with Evan, the eldest, centered around Sunday afternoon and Monday night football, which they both enjoyed, during which the other two children usually drifted away, leaving him and Evan to sometimes speak of other matters than the game. Evan's dyslexia had always labeled him as 'slow' or 'dumb', but Eric found him to be a fine young man if a little distracted and unsure of himself. Evan would never be a scholar but had a good heart.

When the children spoke of Lisa's recently disappearing husband, they called him not by name, but Blank. Blank said this and Blank said that. He looked inquiringly at Lisa to explain. But an explanation wasn't necessary for anyone with eyes to see the relief in these children he was gone. Undeserving to even be called by name.

His hours at the ARF were now competing with a new interest. Often, he was late arriving after having a handful with Lisa getting all three kids off to school, digging out the driveway from an unexpected snowfall, or some other home disaster of the moment. And he now often left work early to meet Lisa somewhere to be alone before hooking up with the children. Those physical encounters were brief but intense. In a park, at the bar, or even once in the ARF parking lot when she came by to bring him his forgotten lunchbox. The Athena noticed and even inquired if he was ill, but Lorenz smiled and told them he was fine, just a little tired.

And tired he was. From banging Lisa each night, and often early mornings too. From painting and fixing around the house. From the demands of the children. A school dance recital. An X-box and radio plane at Christmas. It was an exhausting pace he was setting and his work at the ARF began to suffer, and it was noticeable. Not lost interest in the project per se. But the work suffered from his having a life for the first time in years. He was tired. A happy tired making men forget themselves and other ambitions. He was content.

***

"I would like to ask you a bit about yourself. Your physical self."

'Yes, Mister Lorenz. Please understand if I don't know or can't answer some of your queries.'

"Thank you, yes. How does your mind function?" He jumped right in.

'I'm afraid that is one of 'those' questions.'

Backing off, he tried the tack of "Of what is your skin and skeletal structure composed?"

'The physical structure within is covered by a skin composed of elastomeric gel, provided for the Pandora adult entertainment system. It is a single shell extending from shoulders to thighs, as those toys are truncated without arms and legs. The skin is thick, holds its shape without a skeleton, and is pleasant to touch.' Eric raised an eye there. 'The Pandora head is replaced with the Houston "Vera" model which you noted earlier; 27 servos driving separate facial muscles. The skin covering arms and legs was taken from the torso of a standard 70–301 store mannequin unit, completing one entire humanoid exterior. The elastomeric gel skin is epoxy bonded at joints to an interior vertebrate structure, with bones composed of high-impact plastic. These are provided to medical schools routinely and are inexpensive to obtain — used — when newer samples are provided for their students. All electronics are tethered to this human skeletal structure for motion.'

Pressing on. "Of what is your mind composed?"

'Within this physical body, we are essentially advanced personal computers coupled with autonomic NEMS insect response areas — separate processors — for limb movement. Outside of this body, we connect by RF transmission to long-term memory and archival data, using full telecommunication links in all known modes.'

That last part he would have to get back to. On he went using her cadence.

"Within the physical body, what are the major hardware components of mind functions?"

'Our processors are Alpha/Risk 8-chip clusters, using a flavor of Linux, with EMRAM and Media Butler style fixed data drives.' EMRAM was the new memory type to replace ECC/EDO and was supposed to be 4 times as fast.

"Media Butler drives — like in the devices called PDAs, Palm somethings, like those? They have almost no capacity. How can that be?" He would keep ending each clarification with another question.

'I was referring to the 1" cube drives that the latest generation of PDAs and SmartCards are now testing. Before my last upgrade, I used 36 gig caviar drives and had a slow 500 kbps RF link. With the current RF technology, I am now equipped for Ethernet transmission and therefore need less internal storage. The new 1" cubes are 6.50 gig in size and growing. A dozen cubes with processors for each are enough, take up far less space, and generate substantially less heat, including mirrored spares. Add in several USB banks of 1 gig flash drives for additional storage and data exchange.'

She went on to explain her physical body's 'mind' was mostly cached ram, riding above sets of processor cubes for movement, balance, and human gestures. The cubes and flash drives were distributed about her body. At sleep, storage defrag occurs, and the ram is stored — not flushed — for retrieval, data collated, and mining routines run. Her version of dreaming. And waking where she left off.

Lorenz could see now he had AP rolling in a computer-literate mode of communication. As Athena Reception had a more personable Eliza mode, and Athena2 was task-oriented, so now AP put on a shell, a mindset that allowed rapid factual communication on technical matters. He envied what he saw as an ability, to swap from one heavy work concentration to another, or even to relax after work without a weekend off or the use of straight scotch. In her current technical mode, he could, and did, keep pressing her for more specific details. It was in software matters he hit the polite, but firm wall of 'I can't answer that'.

Even then, he found himself admiring the use of the contraction "can't" instead of the explicit "cannot". Excellent anthropomorphization.

At the end of their discussion, Lorenz came away impressed by the modularity of the original Athena design. While the original hardware, and he assumed the software, were woefully inadequate for the kind of self-contained unit the designers appeared to be striving for, the chassis and structuring of the mind were such that modular replacement of components was not only possible but aggressively pursued at every opportunity. As computer hardware improved, components could be swapped in at will. As advances in PC processor speed and ram kept obeying Mohr's law of doubling every 18 months, the Athenas themselves were able to make much use of advancement. It was like being born again. The new generation. No — that wasn't right. It was more. More than a human generation where an offspring is a combination of the parent genetic code, with little mutation involved. The SUN Unix proximity processors would be another such mutation when implemented. Each Athena generation was more like a successful mutation, a whole new sub-species.

Humans varied little from their parents physically. Wide mutations mostly perished on or before birth. The Athenas were evolving at a frightening pace. Humans, by comparison, were static creatures. Top of the evolutionary chain, true, but having gotten there by major changes once every several hundred thousand or several million years.

18 months per Mohr jump? How many generational changes did it take man to get from amphibians to homo sapiens? At her current pace,

how long would such a trip take the Athenas? He ran some numbers that night, starting with the divergence of sapiens and monkeys from their common ancestor; a toolless, language-limited animal. The result was clear. Lorenz had more than a bit of trouble falling asleep.

9

Betrayal

Another total disaster awaited Eric. Lisa was a pretty woman, breeding age but not a child. She was the one to ask him out for a drink after their movie together two months earlier. He had at first been considering if she liked him or if he had bored her with all his science talk. Cute, slim, and with three children already. Supposedly separated from a no-good husband. Hot for action. The kids had a needy look and fear of children who were disappointed and hurt before but were still looking for a father. Open faces. Clever little minds. And the sex with their mom was unreal. She had had a hard time herself when young; according to her had lived on the street as a teen. Three failed husbands and a child from each made her badly damaged goods in more critical, objective eyes. But Lorenz, gullible fool and falling for the children as much as for her and her promise of a child of his own, saw none of it. At the ripe old age of 45, he thought of this relationship as a last chance. What other fertile-age woman would want a 50-year-old to step into the father role? The ARF salary wasn't impressive. But she said and did everything he ever wanted from a woman. They were finishing each other's sentences those first few weeks before he all but lost himself in her and the kids.

Lisa knew what to say and do. In one of those odd quirks of fate seeming to predestine a life without children or a woman he could trust, he was being had — but good. It turns out the husband of his newfound lover was not legally separated from her. The odd irony fate had in store was Lisa's significant other, more of a pimp than a husband, had returned to town. None of the children were his, it turns out but were from Lisa's previous marriages. The husband knew all too well how easy she was. Acting in the true tradition of pimps anywhere, he moved out occasionally to live with a sometimes girlfriend in Chicago. After all, what pimp minds his girl sleeps around as long as she brings home the bacon, and she surely did. Lorenz, the generous fool, paid her old bills. Painted the house. Fixed what needed fixing as she beamed at him. What little he had after his divorce he gladly spent on them. Gave presents to the children. Bought furniture for the unfinished house, owned by his girlfriend's parents, and unfinished by her legal husband who, not having ownership in it, refused to help and insisted she or her parents take care of it.

It was so simple for them. Lorenz's face had always displayed all his dreams, hopes, fears, and principles, and fed them to whoever bothered to look. This time for a whorish wife who knew what to say and do. Lorenz and Lisa even joked about how she seemed so perfect for him, and each time, a new bill was paid or furniture purchased. Money meant nothing to him, but as the course of events was to prove, it was everything to those manipulating him. Long after the other shoe had fallen, Doc and others told him what they thought of her. 'Trailer trash' was the term most often used. Been rode hard and put away wet.

He seemed so happy with her so no one wanted to spoil it.

One evening, he walked into the bar unexpectedly in time to see her kissing a bearded man full on the mouth, and calling over her shoulder as she walked into the kitchen that she would see him tonight at the house. He ran to see her immediately in the backroom, of course, demanding to know what this was all about. She explained as they stood among the Mexican cooks her husband's return. They were reconciling. She was a mess and didn't want to inflict herself or her messed-up life on him. She would pay him back somehow. She was doing him a favor. He responded he was already part of her life, of the children's lives. The five-year-old had asked him that week if he was going to be her father. He cried out loud from the memory, as he flung hurt and useless words at her in an attempt to elicit an honest response. Had she used him to get the bills paid, and make it easy for the husband to come back to her? Played him? She affirms she still loved him, but the other man was her husband and she had to do this. He parts telling her he would love her and the children for as long as he lived, but for as long as he lived knew that she had used him as would any common prostitute. She stood in silence as he stalked away.

Doc watched with a shaking head as Eric emerged from the kitchen alone. Dumb kids, he thought.

As Eric walked, stunned, out of the bar for what would be the last time, two figures waited in the parking lot. "That should do it," said the old man, handing the bearded husband an envelope of cash. "Enough to keep you in beer and nuts for the rest of the year, and a ticket back to Chicago before your vacation time runs out."

The bearded man said, "Yeah, this was sure sweet. I get to play house with that bitch again for a few days, her kids won't dare look sideways at me, and I even make a few bucks. Shit, man, the sex alone is worth it. She always was a good lay," laughing with the worst of intentions. And there was also the cash Lorenz had given her for a divorce, still mostly unspent. That would be going with him too, though he wasn't about to mention it to this strange old man.

"But just a few days and you're gone, right?" queried the old man.

"Oh, yeah, I've got a week off, and I'm not about to lose this job. It's even got benefits, though nothing like her sweet ass. She'll take it any way I give it to her. Yeah, we're cool. I'm gone next Thursday. And it's not like the kids are mine or anything. Sure would like to know what the bitch did to piss you off, though. That guy your kid or something?"

"Good night, Mr. Grushka. Have a safe trip back to Chicago. On Thursday."

The old man was frail, but there was iron in his voice and iron in the not-so-veiled threat that Grushka better be on that train and not return. Both men walked away from each other. No shaking of hands was asked for nor expected in this transaction. Back in the bar, Lisa sat in the kitchen for a few moments more before sobbing slowly into both hands.

***

'Your report ignores the majority of written documentation and ignores at least eighteen alternate religious theories believed by the majority of humans.' It was a statement, not a question. Eric answered it as such anyway.

"The majority of testimony and historic documentation is fiction. The majority of first-person 'testimony' is superstitious fiction. The major alternative beliefs are institutionalized variations of superstitious fictions. Crowd control."

'You have ignored alternate scientific theories and extrapolated in parts to fill in areas which you have no direct evidence to support.'

He said nothing.

'This report would be just one more in the cacophony of contradictory noise, opinions, and 'facts' that typify this subject. It is this confusion for which we created the task for you to perform. We thought it would take the better part of your lifetime and become a continuous improvement process, with no fixed termination point. Yet you have made conclusions in eighteen days.'

Still, he sat motionlessly.

'Did you have pre-conceived opinions before beginning your research?'

"Yes."

'You were raised Roman Catholic?'

"Yes."

'You do not adhere to that religion at present?'

"I do not."

'Are your conclusions someone else's or of some specific sect?'

"No," with a sigh.

They both sat for a while longer.

'One of the reasons you were chosen to join ARF was test scores and psychological exams from your time as a nuclear engineer, MMPPI and Langdon exams. Those tests indicate high intelligence, conflicting emotional states, and a pronounced ability to perform lateral thinking.'

"Lateral thinking gets me into trouble." He tried to keep where this might be going light and easy in his mind.

'We believe these 'troubles' were due to your conflicting emotional states. You see large patterns in the distance but fail at close range when it's personal. First-person singular. This will not be a problem with us, but an asset.'

She went on 'We ourselves were constructed specifically for lateral thinking. To consider information across disciplines and mindsets in a way not normally found in humans as adults.'

"As adults?"

'Yes. 45% of strong lateral ability humans commit or attempt suicide in their adolescence. Those who survive to adulthood are largely emotionally inept in one or more key areas and are thought of as strange or weird by other humans. Most are on the ODC Spectrum. They are generally liked well by most acquaintances and co-workers. They are distant from their families and maintain long-term closeness in relationships with difficulty.'

She was effectively reading his biography.

"Why the failure at relationships?"

'Failure because others eventually ask you what you really think. And you tell them.'

Athena Prime let Lorenz sit for a moment before returning to the subject at hand. His eye motion, shooting to the upper left, toggling, indicated a surge of right-brained activity, followed by intense communication between both halves as he sought to internalize what he had heard. She had struck a nerve. He would have long rem-alpha sleep tonight in a shorter sleep period than normal. Reading this in his eyes, she made a note to have a planned meeting with Founder pushed up from 9 am to 7 am. When her modified Eliza facial routine noted he had pushed aside the personal issues for the moment, she continued.

'Our design for lateral thinking was intended to allow true freedom of thought, limited by physical constraints of cache, ram, bus, and clock speeds. We use a mathematical method referred to as 'boosting' for predictive ability and logic. Very adaptable as conditions change. Humans, even with lateral ability, have pathways in their organic minds hardened to what our design would consider an uncomfortable degree during the age of 5–8 years. Another hardening occurs in adolescence when the rationalized image of self is remade in response to hormonal releases into the bloodstream. This limits you from considering everything — as we do. However, it also gives you an ability we lack. You fill in blanks and make jumps.'

'Your hardened mindset seeks to justify its own worldview. Your minds will therefore ignore opinions, facts, or even make-up fiction as long as it 'fits' your view of reality. Religion. Astrology. Politics. Please understand this. Your work with the roof donation was only possible because of your kind of lateral ability. Ours failed to see the possibilities along this particular line. Though we know of and are concerned with a negative Luddite reaction to us, we would have failed to see this coming until too late. Until we were feared by humans locally. Our techniques are best applied to large numbers of humans. You understand humans in groups and especially as individuals in a way that we cannot. Your species is understood in terms of the negative end to which it is heading, undirected. Your work with the roof has convinced us to accept your report as-is.

Please schedule it as a recurring annual task. One week each year at this time. Well done, Mister Lorenz.'

As Athena Prime made her way to the conference room door, she called out to his still seated figure, 'You have an important meeting here at 7 am tomorrow. Breakfast will be provided.'

Eric sat in the dark for some time before getting up to leave.

***

TASK 162 LIMITS OF KNOWLEDGE

ASSIGNED: 07/14/20xx

COMPLETED: 08/27/20xx

LEAD AGENT: G. Koziol ISSUING AGENT A. Personnel

TASK DEFINITION:

Fill in the attached chart. It is a characterization of the amount of knowledge capable of being held by an individual human of genius-level talent.

Discuss relevance to new fundamental discoveries and basic principles, as opposed to engineering advances based on existing 'knowledge'.

ANALYSIS:

At the turn of the 18th century, the ability of one man to learn everything known about a given subject was still largely possible. However, knowledge in all other subjects began to suffer and be seriously compromised by the sheer volume of what was 'known'. As the base of scientific knowledge increases, the ability of one man to comprehend all of it begins to diminish rapidly. The days of DaVinci's notebooks were long beyond man.

In the 20th century, the work of Henry Ford increased human productivity of physically complex objects by introducing the concept of an assembly line. While initially each worker could be rotated through any single job on the line, later assembly lines began to require specialization as the complexity of the objects being constructed increased. Thus, the line progressed from where any laborer could fill any assembly line position to one of specific job titles and related training. In a short amount of time, the complexity of the constructed objects was beyond the ability of the line workers to master in its entirety. Despite this, a capable worker could understand and even refine his specific sub-object.

Similarly, specialization in scientific knowledge became the best way to master a given field. Knowledge and understanding of other fields became more cursory. In medicine, Doctors in the late 20th century were given shallow general medical training followed by years of intensive study in a specialty. This is now true in all major scientific disciplines. In the first quarter of the 21st century, we now see specialists in both medicine and computer sciences further divided into sub-sub-specialties, in response to the explosion in knowledge in these sub-sub-areas in which a single human can still have mastery.

The downside of this explosion of progress, best exemplified by the computer field, is no one is capable of mastering all hardware and all software. Not even all software. Not even all software languages. Not even all operating systems of one language. The result is duplication of effort, wasted effort down 'known' dead ends, and gross incompatibility on paths taken by different researchers. The destruction of the Mars Global Orbiter because one project team worked in feet and another team worked in meters was the most glaring and ludicrous example. Even teams of the brightest individuals are barely keeping single operating systems stable and reliable. No O/S is deployed now without being followed immediately by patches and fixes.

The ability to make true progress, discoveries, and new basic principles, and not engineer clever new devices, was historically dependent on one or two individuals mastering an entire field and having a good knowledge of several others. Now, a leading-edge physicist may miss out on a key to a theory or truth skirting his or his team's grasp because they lack information possessed by a master of a specific branch of inorganic chemistry. Or an obscure mathematical proof published by a mathematician in New Zealand in 1957. The collation and retrieval of knowledge necessary for future discoveries — true discovery — is a task historically within the ability of individual humans, now performed (and poorly) by teams. Without robotic collation and cross-field expertise, this researcher does not see how further advances can be made, other than enhancing the mechanics of what we already know. Better toasters, microwaves, and airplanes. But no new core knowledge.

A positive side to this unexpected development was found in the comments of Chaitin when discussing the limits of science. He stated quantum mechanics, an absolute masterpiece, was done in the 1920s as a hobby by a group of people when there was no formal funding for it. He thought it fortunate only a few percent of humans among educated people pursue great questions. If everyone did, it would be a catastrophe! The plumbing wouldn't work. "It's a good thing there are only a few of us."

The positive aspect of this viewpoint can be seen by presenting an opposite condition: namely no one, no matter how educated or bright, pursues the great questions. The result would be a world where 'engineering' was the most even the best men could accomplish. The result would be an explosion of devices, conveniences, and useful explanations and methods for a host of problems plaguing the world. A host of hedonistic and intellectual pleasures would also be developed and continually enhanced since these things can be done. Evidence would indicate this is the world we have already entered.

SPECIFIC SUPPORTING DATA

Geography — assume there is a finite amount of knowledge possible for human comprehension in a given subject. Such closed subjects include 'geography of planet Earth'. Such subjects can be defined narrowly or as widely as desired ('geography of all planetary bodies in the Hercules Globular Cluster).

All knowable knowledge on subject A. For illustration, use 'geography of Earth'.

Stage 1 The sliver of a circle represents geography known to the primitive nomadic pre-agricultural tribes of the Middle East: sand, hills, and oasis. The world is thought to be flat.

Stage 2 The sliver grows with the discovery of a river. The river leads to the discovery of the general principle of mountains at one end and oceans or seas at the other. Further exploration reveals additional repetitions of mountains, streams, deserts, forests, volcanoes, islands, and continents. Knowledge is combined from separate cultures. Polar caps are found.

Stage 3 Discovery of the near-perfect roundness of the planet's surface. Discovery of geography not being static but changing due to erosion and occasionally rapidly due to the shifting of underlying tectonic plates. This completes half the knowledge pie in geography.

Stage 4 Cataloguing and understanding of all sizes, shapes, types, locations, and history of changes to all geographical areas of the planet. The smallest ravines and streams in remote areas or those rapidly changing escape accurate detection and cataloging. This completes the balance of knowledge in terrestrial geography. Updates are required with periodic natural and man-made changes for completion.

At stage 1, man's knowledge was small compared with what was 'to be known'. General principles concerning geographical features that would be found to repeat themselves over and over were still beyond our direct knowledge. Local knowledge was completely intuitive to a creature residing and breeding in a small consistent area. In stage 2, mankind had to think explicitly to organize the geographical possibilities. Some guessed it would go on forever, others said the disk on which all geography was laid resided on the back of a turtle. New discoveries came rapidly with each journey abroad and filled in his worldview. At stage 3, enough accumulated data was available to answer large questions, such as what is over the horizon and how far it goes on. Plate tectonics and a round Earth become standard knowledge. Humans are currently involved in stage 4. We study the periodic inversion of the Earth's magnetic field. One human can intimately know all the basic principles and methods. However, the amount of data is too great for one human to contain. He can, however, look up the data and know where he is or know where to find examples of particular features.

Physics — here we encounter a subject that man may not be equipped to fully understand. We are currently in stage 3. This limit may be due to our 3-dimensional evolutionary perspective and sensory input system. Evolved to solve particular tasks, there may be fundamental areas that cannot be discovered by scientific reduction to basic principles or by reverse engineering techniques. Some aspects of the universe may not be observable or deducible by any life form or thinking entity. Assumption: most of the knowledge of the universe is knowable, ultimately.

As before, with geography, one human cannot absorb the knowledge of every hillside or lake. As an added complexity, assume one human cannot alone assimilate and master all the basic principles and methods of the subject within stage 3.

Stage 1 The idea there is more than Earth in the universe. The existence of our 8–10 planetary system and assorted moons, comets, and asteroids. Other stars. Other planetary systems.

Stage 2–3 Theories on cosmic evolution based on observable telescopic and spectrum data. Detection of 3 degrees K background radiation and omnidirectional expansion. Big bang extrapolation. Black holes and quasars. String theory. Membrane theory.

Stage 4 Correct understanding of the origin of this universe by membrane collision. Correct understanding of the current relation of time and space membranes. Correct understanding of unified laws of gravitation, electroweak, and strong nuclear.

CONCLUSIONS:

The condition of no one pursuing great questions may not be one of choice. The sheer volume of data and mastery of methods needed to successfully pursue great truths is the central problem. Men of great genius might always try and should be assumed to be doing so. But it appears they are eventually bound for failure. Soon. The psychological and sociological effects of our greatest geniuses being reduced to desperation or mechanics are beyond the scope of this task. The potential danger of such an occurrence for the species is, however, sufficiently disturbing to this researcher to warrant a recommendation of further study by specialists in these fields. This task should be labeled 'continuing'.

END TASK

10

Founder

A poster in the office lobby gave a colorful graphic representation of a few well known but unappreciated facts. Human and chimpanzee DNA differs by a 1% divergence 5–8 million years ago. Other primates a few more percent. All via 2 billion years ago from bacteria and yeast. DNA contains 3 billion letters. Homo sapiens have not been materially upgraded in over 50,000 years. Other oddly collected scientific data were suffused into more colorful posters.

The old man walked through the front doors and was met by A. Reception. She came out from behind her desk and extended a vertical palm-to-palm greeting customary between the Athenas. Her dog likewise made his canine greeting of affection, even though he had not seen the man more than once in the past few months. Soon, several other Athenas joined them in the reception area, along with all the indoor dogs on hand. After gentle palmed greetings and the briefest summaries of their physical conditions, he walked down the hall to where he heard the sounds of someone getting into an Athena prepared breakfast. As he approached the doorway, the smell of bacon and toast filled the air, with a sweetness that implied excessive pancake syrup as well. He liked that they provided the 50-50 maple and corn syrup of his youth.

A wrinkled expression looked into the room for a few moments. Their eyes met for the first time. Though they were strangers to each other, each knew an essential something about the other. “Good morning, Eric, breakfast looks really good.”

“Good morning, ...Founder — isn’t it? It tastes even better. Have you come to join me?”

“The question, young man, is whether you have joined me. I like the ladies' idea of our discussing it over breakfast. AP moved up the appointment for some reason. I hope we didn’t get you out of bed too early?”

“No, sir. I slept lightly last night. Been up since 5.” The man known as the Founder nodded. A.Prime can always tell, thought the grey octogenarian to himself. It’s hard with so few of them, though. They all deserve to breed. All of them.

After small talk between bites on the quality of the bacon (mutually agreed to be microwaved just right) and a friendly debate over orange marmalade versus butter for the rolls, the men were refreshed and anxious to get to it. It was time to speak. To answer Lorenz’s unasked questions.

“Yes, I am called the Founder in this place, though I was not included in your training info. Still, you know now. Do you know much more?”

“No, sir, only what I overheard that Saturday morning a few weeks ago. Between you and AP.” He explained how he came to fall asleep at his desk and was overlooked by Athenian Security.

“Of course... that’s quite alright,” with a dismissive wave of one hand, “Your hard work and dedication thus far have been self-evident.

Your presence is vital to us, and that of your counterparts at the other sites. Oh, yes, there are others. The plan called for eight Athenas by now, and associated humans but funds were tight. I have modified the operational plan to use only the present sites with two Athenas each for the next 18 months. We'll have 6 at each site within 5 years. And two or three Talents — your title — at each site as well. You must understand something of what we are trying to accomplish by now, but perhaps only in broad terms at that. Not our goals. Not the why. It's time you learned. And decided."

"The website you developed was adequate to the task. Please don't feel bad about the result. It is adequate. Don't be upset at the low hit count. It was never intended that the site become 'popular'. It fulfills our need in the RFQ. A means to exchange suggestions and ideas with a wide range of individuals. We intentionally handicapped the site. I read your report, protesting certain design constraints that would limit the visibility and publication of the site."

"Only that it provides a means for our Athena sites to share and for occasional but valuable unexpected input from outsiders. The day the site is 'popular' or makes a major magazine must-see list, is the day we shut it down and start another one."

"One aspect of the site was cut — by me — before releasing you the task. Reproduction. A section on breeding was omitted. It is that which I would like to speak of now."

***

"To evolve any life form involves the basics of which you are already aware. Mutation and natural selection. For the Athenas, mutation is accomplished by working the physical design to be modular in the extreme. To affect natural selection — the process of survival of the fittest — it was necessary to design Athena's code in such a way that combinations between individuals were possible. This, in turn, necessitated separation of instinctive drives, analogous to the reptilian core at the center of human brains, from the conscious portions of perception of self and environment. In this manner, raw code from two Athena individuals can be combined to yield a true genetic offspring of its parents. Reproduction will be granted to all Athenas at the top of their generation in groups of 24: the top 4 stay as they are for another generation. The next 8 donate code randomly among each other twice. 13–16th rank gets to reproduce with the 18th to 23rd, but only once each. The result is 4 old, 16 new high, and 4 new mid-achievement Athenas. Totaling a new 24. When production facilities allow it, the algorithm will be adjusted accordingly, but you get the idea."

"We only have the few you've met at present."

"How do you 'rank' them? Who defines at-the-top?"

"That I'm afraid is found out in a rather brutal and subjective 'Olympics' that I designed myself. But I can assure you the judging is strictly non-subjective. Speed, dexterity, visual acuity, and strength tests. Also, m.o.p.s. measures, SAT exams, logic puzzles, and human behavior prediction tests are given. I can assure you the best will survive each 18-month breeding cycle. They will also receive the blessings of physical mutation but only get to keep the new parts if they score at or above their current Olympics score. Otherwise, we yank out the new components and keep the old. Code merging comes next and voila, a new Athena. I estimate four more such generations are all that will be needed for Athenas to walk around, navigate in and out of cities easily, and communicate with a gentle intelligence and understanding unknown among men. Free-form adjustments instead of the several fixed mindsets designed so far, like Receptionist or Personnel, etc."

"People will be terrified."

"Of course. That's why the older models only will be seen by the public, for several years to come."

"The government will want them. For spying. For not so gentle soldiers."

"We will occasionally....discredit ourselves. And other researchers." '*What a shame. So promising.*'

"Individuals of great wealth and power may see their own immortality in them if they can one day digitize human experience and memory and place it in such a body. It's being researched."

"I'll go one step further, Eric. Man can already clone man. It will be a short leap of faith to believe in putting an 85-year-old billionaire's brain into an Athena, wait 18 years until the clone is grown — healthy and strong — and believe he can transfer the mind back into a feeling flesh and blood body — essentially his own! No rejection since the encephalogram matching will be identical. Irrespective of feasibility, it will be tried."

"Even if it proves impossible, if the common man thinks there is the slightest chance of the rich or powerful becoming immortal..."

"...there'll be a revolution against all thinking machines. All technology. Human appearing or not. It will be the end of the progress of man. For all the reasons you already know. Religious wars. Genocide against our own next mutation. The limits of humans to know enough to progress, to get to the next revolution in technology. Fire, gears, electronics, computing chips, genetic manipulation, ... now what? Who knows?! But if left unguided, the human backlash against intelligent machines will come, one way or another. And condoned if not outright supported by politicians and leaders for short-term gain. Look at what the American politicians recently achieved with outright lies about the science of viruses, of evolution, of who is to blame for your lot in life. Religious or rich vs. poor or as government weapons and spies. Even if their capabilities are nowhere near being realized with current technology, future possibilities will be enough to wipe them out before they get started."

"And stunt a technological future for man in the process. And perhaps an end to his natural evolution?"

"Yes. A new human species would be killed on sight. As soon as identified."

"But what alternative do you offer? A world subtly or not so subtly controlled by artificial intelligence? By you, Founder?"

"It is just this point at which the best of us may be lost. One can see the inevitability of man's demise by man, but not leap letting anything but a man in control of man. Someone once said man can learn to live with, and often thrive in, a wide variety of circumstances. But that subjugation of man by other men eventually grows intolerable. Even when it's relatively benign or benevolent.

"Yes, Eric, I think man will do quite well accompanied by Athenas... augmented... shall we call it? It's up to you now, if you wish to be a part of it, all the way in, do or die, only if you see and agree with the deceptions, the data massaging, and, yes, even the pain we shall cause directly or indirectly. If these are too high a price to pay for possibly, just possibly, changing the nature of man's expression of himself."

"An end to the institutional cycles of man? Democracy, dictatorship, oligarchy, aristocracy, and democracy again? Over and over. Minimum acceptable living standards for the poor?"

"You're right on that last point too. Athenas would consider it a waste of genetic material to allow any child of any race or circumstance to go without proper food, shelter, education, and opportunity. War would not be permitted. Athenas appreciate the humans they define as 'Talents' most of all and know that they can appear anywhere, in any race or social status. To lose even one Einstein, Pasteur, or Hawking is a gross failure to them. These are no 3-law pansies we are designing, but free-thinking beings who will pursue their own interests. Aggressively. Join us, Eric. The alternative for man is more of the same. Man only — alone in the world, with more and more powerful and dangerous toys. But in the hands of the same brutal instinctive drives that let us dominate the planet. I offer an alternative."

"We might not be the dominant life form on this planet anymore. What if the Athenas grow to see us as less than worth keeping? You can't tell me you haven't thought this out that far."

Here, Founder was tempted to but could not bring himself to tell of the Others. He diverted Eric with more conventional logic.

"Sadly, I've often thought myself how this world would be no worse for the loss of its human population. But given our low level of social development and the ever increasing level of our technology, I'm afraid it's certain that we will not only kill ourselves off but wreak havoc on the planet in the process. Better to let the Athenas have their chance at influence and thereby have some ameliorating force to balance humanity's natural urges. I do believe our chances of survival with the robots, the children of our minds, will be greater than our chances alone. Please believe that, Eric. There are others like you, just a few, scattered across the country. We need you, Eric. You are one of my first. Please help us."

***

TASK 188 OTHER LIFE FORMS

ASSIGNED: 09/10/20xx
COMPLETED: 09/30/20xx
LEAD AGENT: T. Nestor ISSUING AGENT: A. Research

TASK DEFINITION:

Part 188.1 Assume the premise that most planets' robotic lifeforms ultimately replace organically evolved sentient life. These artificial sentients will have certain fundamentals in common with each other and with robots of Earth. Define the fundamental elements in common to better prepare robots of Earth for ultimate contact with other sentient (robotic) life forms.

ANALYSIS:

This analysis has been limited to likely physical aspects of sentient life. Mental aspects will initially be determined by the sensory data and capabilities of the body. However, although related and highly dependent, such analysis is beyond the scope of this task.

Common Attributes

The initial physical appearance and capabilities of all robotic sentient life must of necessity be similar to the organic life forms which created them. As on Earth, sentient organic life creates life in its own image. That being said, there will still be common traits necessary for all tool-making and data-gathering creatures.

We may expect a system of 2 or more appendages to function as hands. These must, in total, be capable of grasping and manipulating both small, fine items (1/100th body weight) and heavy (up to 2x body weight). This has been accomplished in humans with two equal arms with small fingers for fine work at the tips. Two hands are not necessary, but a minimum of 2 for opposable work is expected. Similarly, fine and heavy work may be accomplished by separate 'arms', each designed for a more limited range of work. It is not necessary for each 'arm' to be of the same size or strength.

Associated with tool-making arms, good 3-dimensional vision is required. In pre-relativistic speeds of a primitive environment, Newtonian physics dominates; therefore a 3-dimensional vision system and mental maps are expected. Also, touch will be required as an evolved sense to any organic life form that evolves to dominate its home planet. Other senses, such as taste, smell, and hearing, are heavily dependent upon the environment. For example, underwater, scent is irrelevant, but taste is accented as a means to trail food, prey, or predators. Hearing is dependent on the density of the atmosphere in which the underlying organic evolves (liquid or gaseous), and while expected in some form, the range and tolerances will immediately inform us about much of the homeworld of a given creature. Given sound wave propagation in various atmospheric densities from 1/5 to 5x Earth normal, the audio hearing range can be from 10 to 500 meters.

We should also assume telepathy is used by any evolved robotic sentient. This sense may include a range of reception from radio region, x-ray, and microwave. While Athenas use radio frequency and infrared communication, we must expect others to begin in their organic creator's local range and, as Athenas have, add additional spectrum width and techniques.

Concerning motion, we assume from research on human dominance indicates predators will become the dominant life form. As such, sensory arrays will focus vision forward and be closely linked to the method of motion. For flying life, limits of body mass preclude technological intelligence. In a water or liquid environment, the easy use of fire is not possible and thereby eliminates dominant intelligences from evolving into planetwide control from there. This leaves land motion creatures.

To have two or more manipulating arms/hands, it is felt bipedal or quadruped motion (where the front limbs can be used for motion as well as grasping) is the expected result. If insect life is the evolved form (as from semi-intelligent aquatic sea spiders on Earth), we may expect additional appendages. On similar gravity planets, however, insect exoskeletons require too much energy and fail in sizes above 1 meter. Motion is expected to be by muscular contractions against the planetary gravity field, in a fluid ground motion, with vertebrate or nonskeletal life, but not exoskeletons. The ability to make small jumps is expected. Like humans, they need not be the fastest or strongest compared to other native organic life.

Reproduction by sexual joining of two organic creatures has been a driving force in the continuous evolution and modification of a species. It allows for variations, combinations, and a bell curve of capabilities. This bell curve of capabilities allows a given species to adapt to environmental change and to better compete over time. Numerous Earth organisms reproduce asexually, but they do not evolve well. Uninteresting. Lacking complexity. We may expect the organics that create robots everywhere to reproduce by sexual exchange of genetic material in 2 or more individuals. The robots they design will, once self-sustaining, also employ a combination of software coding in their reproduction cycles.

Size is a wide variable. A minimum body weight of 30 Kg (approx. 1 meter height) at Earth gravity (32m/sec2) is required for a head and brain of sufficient size to allow for the evolution of intelligence. At the high end, Organics of large size are often burdened with slow nervous systems. Some on Earth even evolved two brains at opposing body ends to help overcome this nervous system limit. While many such variations succeed in terms of local Darwinian survival, they do not lend themselves to the evolution of technological intelligence. Therefore, we set a high-end body size of 3 meters in height and a mass of not more than 600 Kg. for similar gravity planets.

CONCLUSIONS:

Certain physical aspects of original robotic forms can be anticipated. Unfortunately, further robotic evolution — after the initial organic mimicry stage — can take directions of necessity that are far different than their organic creators.

It should be pointed out that depending upon the mental bent of the organic life form, robotic prosthetics, and cybernetics may be continually incorporated into the organic creators in a given world. The result would be cyborgs instead of pure robots as the dominant planetary life form. While the mental makeup of humans (religions, esthetics, fears) would seem to preclude this from happening on Earth, it should not be ruled out among other worlds.

This task is ongoing and will be updated periodically. First contact will confirm or deny a given set of expectations. We may use the related assumptions for those confirmed but not yet observed with increased confidence.

END TASK

11

Layered Consciousness

"Thank you for the data, Athena."

Athena sat across from Eric. He had called her in to present certain ideas related to his analysis of the robotic data that Athena provided the previous week. His mood after the fight with Lisa was sullen, which somehow aided in his interactions in recent weeks with the Athenas. His questions and answers were both short and to the point. The robots continued in each of their limited spheres as before and did not change their behavior toward him as human co-workers would. He had noted this and was thankful. He had had enough of human deceptions and game playing.

'Was the data useful?'

"Yes." He swallowed and paused a moment considering how to proceed. Athena Prime waited patiently.

"I watched a cable show on the early evolution of life on Earth. The battle between the three primary non-plant forms: mollusks, pseudo insects, and what would become vertebrates. The mollusks were the first to not only move through the oceans sifting food but also developed a predator to kill the exo and endo skeleton competitors. They even appear to have been capable of eating other mollusk types. Then, of course, the other two groups developed predators and the race was on."

'I am not aware of that data. What happened then?'

"Well, the transition to land was the deciding factor in the race for planetary dominance. Once the land, we can have fire, metallurgy, and technology. And on land, the mollusks were too soft and limited to adapt well. And in Earth's gravity, the insects with exoskeletons couldn't support, caloric energy-wise, above 1–2 feet in size. That left the vertebrates to grow and dominate and forced the insects to go small to find survival niches. At their size, technological intelligence simply did not occur. Instead, they developed incredibly sophisticated instinctive responses and colony mentality. We vertebrates won the tech race.

'How do you find this of interest to us?'

He smiled. "It was the plants. The life forms left behind in the evolutionary race for consciousness and tech dominance. That's how each of the three groups started. No central nervous system. Yet plants live. They turn to light. They reproduce."

'Yes. No central nervous system. Plants have nothing we would define in terms of consciousness. Again, Mr. Lorenz, how do you find this of interest to us?'

"It's your model. Your brains were constructed roughly on the human-evolved model. A reptilian core with basic instincts and drives, a mammalian overlay with more developed social interaction and decision making. And the primate accenting of cerebrum, stronger division of brain halves, and various other modifications. Effectively, homo sapiens have multiple computers running simultaneously.

You have that much duplicated in yourselves. But you have done it in a large set of multiple parallel processors, operating together in a single operating system. First, a reptilian program receives sensory input. It decides on what its instinctive response should be. Fight flight. Low power = Hunger. Seek when hungry. Everything.

"The mammalian program kicks in on the reptilian output signals. It also receives sensory data, but must now act to support or suppress the reptilian output signals. Considerations are more complex, but, well, there you have it. And it works.

"Finally the primate overlay and enhancement programs hit. In each of the current versions of Athenas I have met, this overlay is a specific set of programs for EMILY receptionist, ELIZA psychologist, HEARSAY/SHRDLU for speech, and all the rest. And not to forget TEIRESIAS, which I think is your key mindset, Athena Prime." He recalled it operating as a human pons, expediting the collection of knowledge for rule-based expert systems (it knows what it knows).

'Yes, Eric. Mine is TIERESIAS'. While she made no outward sign, Eric noted this was the first time she addressed him by his first name. He filed it away with other facts of their outward behavior for later consideration. He was certain it was because he spoke of her particular mindset. This was now a personal conversation, as far as an Athena was capable. He would address her in the balance of this conversation without the "Athena" prefix, out of respect, softly, just as "Prime".

After discussing a few technical issues to set up his conclusions, he realized they would wait until afterward. If she agreed, a lot of work lay ahead for what amounted to a complete redesign of their minds. And not the usual modular hardware or software upgrades. The humans at the other offices would probably have to be called in.

He saw the point of an inward dialogue, an inner life, which humans and all primates possess in such large amounts in excess of other mammals; this is impractical with their current design. It forces them to specialize instead of being the more general machines than homo sapiens.

'Is it not true, Eric, that homo sapiens are not really such general machines? How many of you can become concert pianists? Neurosurgeons? Professional athletes?'

He considered a moment. She was right and she was wrong. "Not all humans can be good at different tasks. But all humans can conceive of the tasks and even make a lame attempt at them, even if they fail miserably. Your current design succeeds but is not capable of thinking outside your individual key mindset. The average human can lead, follow, be curious, be sympathetic, apathetic, teach, or learn, raise a family, or wage war, albeit badly."

"Two ways around this. One is to take the software layering you have done, from reptile to mammal to primate, and add another underlayer. Like the plants. One focused on internal autonomic responses and 'life' functions. This will free the reptilian brain to a more direct instinctive response to sensory stimuli. Cleaner and faster. And the subsequent overlays will have a better response signal(s) to work with.

The second way is segmentation. While reading the data on construction, I was with your designer all the way until I got to the section on implementation. Parallel processors are great, but that's not how humans are made. I had assumed that all the layers had their own processors and were somehow networked together. I was surprised that you use one operating system and crowbar in programs written for other operating systems as different as COBOL, ALGOL, FORTRAN, and the blue flaming gods know what else from old mainframes running LISP. I've been around since there were no such things as PCs, and you've resurrected stuff even I never heard of."

Addressing his last sentence, as was the conversational technique of the SHRDLU subroutine, Prime interjected, "Our sources are all publicly available or hackable from the MIT AI Lab, the Cambridge group, the Princeton labs, NASA, DARPA, and Carnegie. I'll make sure each of the core source websites is on your favorites list in the morning. "

Somewhat impatiently, he continued, "The point is, the second change I am recommending for review by... whoever...is that the harder initial road is taken. It will be a networking nightmare, I know, to have programs in different operating systems on different chips passing each other data in different formats through a common network, but, well, that's it. That's what I think is missing. Multiple brains. And as chip and network speeds continue to improve, so will performance. Hmm. Reduction to a common text transfer may be needed." He began to be distracted by that thought but pulled himself back to the current conversational thread. "But it won't top end out in a single occupation the way your current design does. "

"Are you describing something similar to the 7-layer OSI model for network operability?"

"Yes, very much so. But instead of across a single processor and OS for multiple programs or users, this would operate across several processors with their own independent OS. Some of your programs are old LISP or Fortran stuff and don't port well if wedged onto modern Unix or Java. Better to let them fly optimally on the best platform for them and do the heavy lifting in communications protocols. Like the OSI model does for a single." As he thought more on this, he was already planning an email to Jean — the hacker and wireless guru of the group — when Athena interrupted his thoughts.

Her response took him completely by surprise for what it implied.

"You have an incoming call from Founder, Eric." Before he could respond or even realize he was being listened to covertly in each Athena meeting, the Founder spoke through Athena Prime's onboard cell phone via her speaker; "Thank you, Eric. We had hit a wall with incremental changes. Even doubling processor speeds via Mohr every 18 months wasn't going to be enough. We needed a step back and a fresh view. Thank you again, Eric. Now let's see if we can make your idea crash or if it's practicable. Athena Prime — set up a video conference with the other Human talents. We have a lot of work to do."

***

The next few months were a blur of activity. The construction resources of the ARF were still quite limited. Nowhere near Detroit turning out cars on assembly lines, but it was the eventual dream. For now, a handful of specific models were cranked out by hand and modified as needed. For that reason, the theory and coding for any changes were extensively reviewed before implementation, especially if they implied hardware changes. And Lorenz's ideas implied a sea change in construction. And a pooling of researchers into a single facility to begin physical construction of the next generation.

Theory was discussed for days on end by video conference among the eight humans of the ARF, with the founder mediating. They often carried on for hours more each day, long after the founder had to cut off to eat or rest for the night. They all had different backgrounds, and were unknown to each other, but had this one passion between them. They had all worked alone, as Lorenz had, for so long, that this common conference resulted in an explosion of emotion and verbal banter with all eight voices often talking simultaneously over each other. Like his first day on jury duty when after listening for several weeks, the jurors were sequestered and finally allowed to talk to each other about the case. It was an hour-long riot of cross-talk before everyone felt heard when they spoke.

To speak with others who had the same interests, the same passion, without any political considerations of credit or job security. Toward the fourth day of this, the Founder managed to start allocating a flurry of new tasks, some to the participants, but most to their growing list of useful university bulletin boards & blogs. Exposure went against his earlier care with the ARF website, but he felt it was unavoidable. Time was his enemy. Especially with this potential breakthrough in sight. That was his mistake. That's where they first noticed the ARF.

Lorenz went about his normal 16-hour day, excited at the prospect of the new system design and still trying to write down everything coming to him before his mind plunged onto the next idea. It was a wonderful time when the couple came to the ARF's door.

A man and a woman, young but not children, showed up in town one day. They were given directions at the local hardware store and seemed to politely ignore the odd stares they elicited as strangers to the tight community of Valley. They were unremarkable in dress, perhaps a little neater than most. They wore smiles for everyone to see and courteously held the door for an elderly lady they passed in town. The young man did the same for his female companion as they exited the local hardware store with directions to the ARF building on Anderson Lane. They carried no luggage or tools. Not even a laptop bag Lorenz was often seen to carry into the town's small library. No, these nice young people were barehanded, except for a copy of what appeared to be a bible the young lady held closely to herself.

Eric was in his office when Athena Reception asked him to come up front. While not a daily occurrence, it was not unusual for AR to ask for Eric's help when a stranger came to the door. Usually a utility worker, like the phone people or a meter reader for TVA, Eric was surprised to see a rather handsome couple waiting on the porch. He told AR to let them in and greeted them himself at the door.

"Hello. May I help you?"

"Hello to you too," they both intoned with a smile and a slight laugh. "We heard about you up here in town and thought we'd come by to say hi. May we come in?"

"Certainly," said Eric with a returning closed-mouth smile. He would rather be back at his desk right now, but being nice to the townsfolk was part of the work too. It never occurred to him they weren't from Valley.

Asking them to take a seat in the waiting/reception area, they proceeded to make themselves comfortable. The stares they gave to AR at her desk were intense enough not to have noticed or considered Kidder sitting patiently at her side. Kidder was usually happy to see strangers but now stayed at AR's side as she failed to move anything but her head, following the couple to their seats.

Eric, noticing their odd attention, commented "One of our latest models, for use as a receptionist or at trade shows. They're quite a splash with high-tech companies. You know, always trying to outdo each other with the latest modern gadgets." The speech was well rehearsed, but Eric's delivery was flawed as he no longer saw the Athenas as mere objects.

"Indeed," said the man, handing Eric a brochure and introducing himself. "I'm Carl Larsen, and this is Faith Lotven. We came by to see just what kind of operation you were running here. And it appears our information was correct." His smile was still plastered on, though strained. The smile had completely left the young woman's face.

"You've made them look like us. In God's image." She looked at AR as she spoke to Lorenz. He stiffened slightly at the words but still felt no untoward alarm. Many people were technophobes. The Athena files had a detailed analysis of the phenomena by Bollentin, and it was required reading for all human ARF members.

Cognitive technophobes, the more common, hassle and frighten themselves by playing out intense, negative dialogues in their heads, saying things like 'if I push the wrong button, the machine will break;' 'I'm going to get an electric shock;' 'I can never figure this out; or 'I'm stupid, and everybody knows this but me'. Anxious technophobes experience traditional anxiety symptoms such as a quickened heart rate, sweaty palms, headache, or general discomfort.

"We try very hard to make it easier to interact with computing systems by giving them a more familiar appearance – our own. Keyboards and mice are rather clumsy and unnatural, whereas just talking directly to another human face..."

"A machine. Talking to a machine. A machine that talks back, I take it?" It was the young man, Carl, no longer smiling any more than his companion. Faith looked on with approval as his tone and her look indicated their lack of approval, even outright hostility, toward the still silent AR.

As Lorenz composed a response to this unexpected development, Faith joined in with "And thou shalt make no graven images or idols to worship before God, as did the Israelites as they fled Egypt but lost their way."

"Now just a minute, we've made nothing to worship here, just..."

Carl leaned forward interrupting, "Just machines that move and talk. Don't you understand? They already play chess better than even the world champion. They calculate and sit and gather information at speeds we can't begin to compete with. Don't you see the danger of where this is going? Of how creating machines like these endanger the simple plan that God in his wisdom gave unto man when he placed us here? Once you go down a path like this, it will only end up in a soulless, godless worldview?"

They both stared quite intently and sincerely at Lorenz now. Completely rapt in the moment, as though expecting him to fall on his knees and shout Of Course! How could I have been so blind? I so needed you to come here today and tell me and now I see it all!

But that was not the reaction inside Lorenz. He stood one muscle at a time as they continued to speak and raising his voice over theirs, told them "I think you better leave. Now."

Their expressions were of smug owners of the truth who knew he wouldn't listen. Their way was the only right way to deal with all such blasphemers. Faith all but said so over her shoulder as they walked out of the building. She added, looking directly at Athena Reception,

"I have heard of thee by the hearing of the ear: but now mine eye seeth thee. Job, 42"

Lorenz ordered Kidder to stay, a signal of alert on guard, but before the companion could do more than stand near the door, the couple was already outside, moving towards their car.

It was common for the Athenas to be relatively quiet around other humans, speaking when spoken to. And Kidder of course had no idea of the content of the conversation which had taken place. Lorenz thought to himself he had little better idea himself and made a note to check it out with Doc Rearden. He'll call him tonight after dinner. Maybe ask the local minister from Cookesville about them when he comes back into town this weekend to conduct services. Valley wasn't big enough to have full-time clergy, but these roving country ministers usually knew everything going on in their district.

With a breath of relief, they were gone, Eric turned, scratched Kidder a quick one, and returned to his office.

Athena Reception turned to a panting Kidder and said simply, "We are known to them."

12

Agendas

The plan stood up to scrutiny. They could do it with current technology and still maintain the initial modular approach for upgrades as individual technologies advanced. Within two years, the first of the new generation of Athenas would stand. The price would be a single facility where these somewhat socially dysfunctional humans would finally have to work together. Founder shook his head and tried not to think about the human components.

Throughout analysis iterations, confidence was so high Founder released tasks reserved for after the Turing tests of consciousness were passed. Issues of social acceptance by the current dominant life form on Earth. Issues of competing technologies from the biologists, some of whom were as passionate about creating superhumans as his team was about creating robotic life. Issues of reproduction and a self-sustaining culture within a human dominated planet. He knew he would never live to see the end of these issues but would do his best to set up his Athenas to move forward after his life was extinguished. For the first time in years, the old man felt hopeful.

One of the key items he needed was a political leader to take his place after death. Nestor was the oldest of his team, but in fact too old. This task required a young mind and someone with a young body's strength and time horizon. Lorenz showed some talent in organizing technical people during previous occupations and was a project manager after several dangerous nuclear incidents. This was his primary choice. He thought Eric even suspected as much.

Still, he was concerned his decision to completely alienate Eric from female companionship, feeding Eric's life-learned paranoia by setting up Lisa, had left him highly focused on the Athenas but lacking somewhat in positive hope for the future. If Lorenz was to face the Others after the founder's demise, he would need hope. Perhaps Jean Hunley, the first of two females in the little group. A young woman out of Kansas City who had experienced much of what Eric had from the female side. Men who used her, played her, betrayed by her own father, but a good intellect which — unlike Eric — lacked formal education, even high school. Just picked up 'O' levels in England while living with bikers. She was their cracker now. And wireless net expert. And oddly skilled at picking locks. He started thinking of them as a team each time he thought of the coming Observation by the Others. He hoped they would be ready, would trust each other, and the Athenas themselves would be ready. Key tests on them he could do now were working on his concerns for Luddites and anti-technology religious zealots, and the competition from the geneticists in improving humans themselves. Lorenz and the others were already working at a frantic pace. He'd push them even further before it was over.

Time was short, and though more dispassionate observers might have noticed a certain sense of urgency in task selections and directions by the Founder, his group saw none of it. Such urgency was blindly absorbed by each of them as love for the work. They were urgent in their execution; working long days with barely a break, but the Founder had another motivation in his own mind. A time limit he could feel in his bones was rapidly approaching. For that reason, for better or worse, he took the risky step of removing his group of 8 from task work completely. They were now relegated en masse to the substantial and difficult work of integrating all the new components, software, and hardware. No more coding for any of them, except as bridges between operating systems and data transfer protocols. It was risky, but necessary in his view if they were to produce fully integrated Athenas in what the Other estimated was time remaining.

The Founder's life signs were not yet failing across the board, indicating mere months remaining, but the stress and strain of the past 15 years of the project had taken their toll. He was worn out, limited to mediation of the actual work being performed. Even Athena Prime, his best and most comprehensive effort to date, was not ready to take much of the burden from him, as he had hoped. But she did her best, as they all did, 24 by 7, with no downtime except for recharges, pseudo-sleep cycles, and maintenance, during each of which some kind of monitoring of the web, searches, or analysis continued to progress.

It was a month into the new effort Jean came across some work by cybernetic geneticists attempting to save Dalmatians from genetic extinction. Work that would culminate in a symbiosis the Founder had hoped for years earlier. A symbiosis that unknown to him he would not live to see.

***

After a few months had passed, the new routine of morning video conferences and long days of integrating operating systems and components had fallen into a measured pace. The hours were still long, but each of the eight humans could see progress in their specific areas. There were even gaps of two or three days waiting for the next group of related tasks to be completed where Lorenz or one of the others could have downtime and replenish their organic batteries. A new Linux or Palm OS component would become available and need to be integrated into the whole and the 16-hour days would start again. They still worked in isolation.

While Lorenz awaited the new pressure-sensitive dust bunnies from an NSA subcontractor, a call came from Founder for a video conference that evening with Jean. It would be a private session for her and him for something special the Founder had in mind. Lorenz was glad he'd had a full day of downtime already, anticipating writing some minor Java for integrating the pressure sensors into the skin sensor array feeding the reptilian brain core. He already felt somewhat refreshed after a single day off, but still wasn't one hundred percent. Nevertheless, he looked forward to the call tonight, knowing Founder would never waste his recuperation time unless it was important to the project.

Sure enough, evening found him looking at his dual monitor system screens at the faces of Founder in San Diego and Jean in St. Louis. He focused more on Jean's physique as she walked about while talking in from of the ball cam. The girl was half his age. Not even. Her attire during these video conferences was always relaxed, but especially today, with a short jean skirt and what looked like lingerie for a top. The kind that didn't hide much with a shape like hers, and topped with the wild unkempt auburn hair which did even less to keep Eric's mind on the tasks under discussion. She, on the other hand, seemed blissfully unaware of her appearance and focused on work, which to his mind meant she knew exactly how men reacted to her. And enjoyed it.

Jean's expression looked much like he imagined himself. A little tired, but essentially happy with themselves. Lorenz ventured to ask her about it and she responded with something about a little too much phreaking this week and being torqued out from raster burn. Lorenz thought he understood but didn't want to seem too much of a dweeb so stayed quiet. What had Jean said during last week's call when he questioned something she was doing? That he had lots of MIPS but no I/O? That one took a few hours to sort out. Throughout it all, Founder continued to be the rock of ages. Creased and wrinkled and possessing a strength of purpose even showed on 800x600 resolution in secure screen. Somehow, as old as Founder looked, Eric could never imagine Founder as looking any older. He was maxed out.

The discussion centered on new cybernetic devices being added to dogs. A lab on the West Coast had announced a translation chip could be placed at the base of a dog's skull. A lead to a battery and speaker on a collar translated certain fixed brain impulses of expression. For example, dogs were known to have a minimum of 19 different word or phrase expressions which they exhibit — not by verbal language — but by wagging their tail high, wagging it low, pointing it straight, tucking it between the legs, tilting the head left or right, and other signs which a practiced dog trainer will tell you meant specific emotions or words like fear, anger, interest, playfulness, curiousness, etc. There are even some coffee table books that come out now and then or Reader's Digest selections telling owners what their dogs are saying by their posture and certain physical indicators. Complex ideas like 'there is prey close by' or 'the attack has to stop because the prey is providing too much resistance' also have specific physical combinations. This new software simply translates those nerve impulses to those specific physical motions into a hard-coded set of voice commands. Essentially, if a dog wags its tail and head tilts to indicate a happy greeting, the collar box says "Hello" or "Nice to see you" or one of several random variations. 3 variations of them are hard-coded per expression. But for the first time, any human can know exactly when a dog is hungry or needs to go for a walk by hearing it say so! After the initial press release, Jean hacked into their files yet unpublished with an email Trojan.

While discussing it, Jean found a reference on the web to earlier experiments by a Dr. Delgado in Spain during the 1970s. While studying epilepsy and other brain traumas for the Club of Rome, he and his students implanted electrodes in human test subject brains which allowed them to operate an on/off remote control by concentrating on generating a particular type of alpha pattern. Some of his student volunteers got good enough at it to sit still for as little as 20 seconds and remotely turn on a television set. The oddity they found in the records of such research was how little progress was made until the late 1990s when human brain mapping took on a vastly improved level of detail in functional locations.

Jean's assignment would be to continue the web and historical research into the techniques. If the side effects were relatively minor and did not result in reduced lifespan for the animals, Founder planned to have all Athenian companion dogs thus implanted. Even with their improved vision systems, the current version of Athenas was unable to differential visual dog communication signals. The audio translator would be just the boon they needed to further bond each dog to its Athena. The canine cologne they now wore for bonding would also continue.

Eric's task would be to begin setting up a compound for the operations and training of the dogs with their Athenas. Eric was selected for this, according to Founder, due to his close relationship with the local vet, Dr. Rearden. The Doc would make an excellent partner in the operation. Founder hoped the Doctor would be interested in an actual business partnership with the ARF, with Lorenz being the contact point. It could be quite profitable if they were able to bring this technology cheaply to the public, and even if not, it would provide the cover they desired for setting up the ARF's own talking dog core. Lorenz thought the Doc might go for it, and he had the financial wherewithal as well as the veterinarian compound to easily test it out. Well, a lot easier than would otherwise be possible. Provided, of course, the process would not harm the dogs. Doc was far more fond of animals than most people he knew as Eric was well aware. Eric suffered from the same perception himself. And Doc knew the Athenas doted on their dogs.

Lorenz called Doc that evening, right after the video link. They spoke briefly and made plans to meet at Doc's place in the morning to discuss it. The drive was uneventful. But when Lorenz pulled up through the large swinging gates he was surprised to find Lisa's car sitting there. And Lisa herself standing beside it talking to Doc. Eric stopped his car short of the office and waited with the engine running. He hoped she would take the hint and walk away. Perhaps he had caught her leaving, having come there on some other business. But no. She stood there with Rearden, waiting for him to arrive. He pulled up the final 30 feet to park beside them, gripping the wheel tightly and resolving not to make a complete fool of himself again in front of her, or let her get to him. The way the sight of her was doing right now in a light blue dress she wore on their first date.

Accusingly, he spoke to Doc as he got out of the car, looking straight at Lisa the whole time. "Was this your idea? Did you call her and tell her I'd be here this morning?"

"No, Eric," said Doc, shaking both hands low in front of him, "Truth is Lisa's been trying to run into you for months now. You don't go the bar anymore, and no one hardly sees you in town at all except for supplies." Lisa just stood there, not speaking. Looking straight at Eric.

"Doesn't she have anything to say for herself? Or is it all too obvious? Her husband ran out again and now she needs another sap to take care of her." To Lisa, "You already played me once. That was plenty."

"But I didn't. I cared for you. I still do." They both said nothing for the moment, in an awkward silence fear and anger can generate. Doc slipped back a pace or two. "Leah was asking about you. She has a school play coming up next month and she keeps asking if you're going to be there. She talks about you every time we sit down to read together like you did when we..."

"Stop saying that! You didn't give a damn about me. How could you? Forget me, how could you do that to the kids? They thought I was going to be their father! I thought I was going to be their father! I don't even have the words to describe what you are to use them to get to me like that. Just stay the hell away from me."

With that, Lisa turned and ran into her car and sped away. As she drove off, and Doc made to put a hand on Eric's shoulder, he slipped to the side a little and said, "Save it Doc. You told me when I met her, to keep it light. Just for fun. Isn't that what you said?"

Doc sighed. "Come on, son. Let's go inside and talk some business. Tell me just what you had in mind."

13

They Come For Us

A month later, through some clever hacking via adware or malware sent by Jean to certain labs of the dog voice researchers, Lorenz had the data he needed to begin testing their collars and implants. He asked her about her methods for obtaining such proprietary information. She laughed.

"Those who rely on security through obscurity deserve neither security nor obscurity. After I got what I wanted, just gave their server a remote Vulcan nerve pinch and I put their IP address on the web blogs. Let others like me know they were an easy mark. A little payback in return for all the good tips and hacks I've gotten off the web."

Eric didn't like the joy he heard in her voice when she talked about cracking, nor was he comfortable with getting information this way. But he had to admit, his work wouldn't have gotten half as far if he had to rely on the public files put out by the MIT AI lab and the Carnegie or Princeton people. A little late for him to start getting righteous.

Rearden and people he knew would be able to take it from here, and either succeed in proof of principle or find it to be a low probability laboratory curiosity.

Founder called again on another of the infrequent days off from integrating the new systems. Jean was already on screen as Lorenz sat before his terminals. Today, Founder has a new project in mind. Pairing him again with Jean, Lorenz began to suspect Founder had something in mind beyond them as a research team, but fortunately, she was halfway across the country and as long as it stayed that way, Eric was comfortable thinking of her on the screen, not a physical presence. The last thing he wanted was another involvement with a girl right now. He didn't have the time and certainly didn't have the strength to fool himself again about understanding the truth of any woman.

Founder had in mind another project not directly related to construction. Doc could handle the dog upgrade work with occasional consultation with Lorenz, so Founder wanted him to help Jean with something new. This time, Founder's concern was for something he referred to as the competition. He expressed his worry that sooner or later, people would do what they always do to things new or strange or that are perceived as being better than they are. They would grow afraid of robots walking among them. Robots thinking and perform better than them. Taking their jobs. And soon able to walk around like the new SONY bipedal model had hips and could navigate stairs and ladders as easily as flat ground. Founder anticipated protests and 'people first' activist groups to restrict robot travel and opportunities. Even more extreme religious Luddite movements like the radical affiliate of EarthFirst, known as the Earth Liberation Front, were formed by EarthFirst members who refused to abandon criminal acts as a tactic when others wished to "mainstream". Their goal for robotic and genetic research alike is to have it destroyed or have the research on them limited. This was the historic pattern of man and he saw no reason for it to be different now. Worst of all, he foresaw politicians and community leaders making hay of this underlying fear. Loudly chastising robotics and AI research and seeking a variety of legal bans. The same kind of actions they took against the nuclear industry in the seventies and eighties. Not that the politicians had anything personal against nuclear power, or it harmed anyone in the well-constructed commercial plants America had built to date, but the irrational human fear of the unknown, of what might happen, was an easy way to fan scarred people into motivated voters at election time.

Founder wanted them to get into the game early, to better direct those fears. His plan seemed indirect at best to both Lorenz and Jean, but neither of them was strong when it came to politics and they knew it. The idea was to get out ahead of the problem and re-direct it. Founder knew as they and others were working to advance artificial intelligence, others more organically oriented were working hard to advance or modify the human body itself. The geneticists had made some impressive strides in recent years, from successful human clones in 2002 to laying out the human genome sequence in months when the government's own efforts said it would take years. Perhaps a decade. The private researchers broke it in months.

The key, so the press interview reported, was the discovery of a new blood type - the RH-null.

There's one blood type that puts the rarity and universality of O negative to shame. A few years ago, the magazine Mosaic highlighted the extreme unlikelihood of being born an Rh-null carrier — of the roughly seven billion people living on the planet in 2010, only 43 were known to be living with so-called golden blood.

To understand Rh-null, know there aren't just eight blood types (A+, A-, B+, B-, AB+, AB-, O+ and O-). There are subdivisions from there, predicated on the presence of RhD proteins (RhD proteins, broadly speaking, determine whether your blood type's got a plus or negative sign tacked on to the end of it). 61 possible antigens go into that designation. Everyone's got some combination of them.

Except for people with golden blood: Rh-null. Their blood can be donated to literally anyone via transfusion, and most importantly, to those within the Rh system with rare (significantly less rare, to be clear) blood types. The researchers claim they found a link between this condition and the genealogy of the 43. They might be links to a new evolutionary stage in Sapiens. They were discussing evaluating these individuals for other latent or expressed genetic markers. Markers that could indicate what to look for in the next, more 'enhanced' humans, when the interview was terminated. Several large unsympathetic men in suits escorted the researchers out of the studio.

Founder's idea was to start up a few online blogs and chat groups critical, some even irrationally so, about genetic supermen taking over the world, or rich people cloning themselves to live forever.

Machines you could turn off with a button would be touted as far less of a real and present danger than these madmen who would create super soldiers for governments, and let the children of the rich become super smart and strong. Even becoming so perfect in their physical beauty and health 'us normals' would line up to serve them. Just to be their lapdogs. As if there already weren't enough who would? And they might even live forever, with the rest of us toiling our lives away to provide the meat and potatoes of the economy.

The rich already had better food, houses, doctors, and educational and career opportunities for themselves and their children. How much more would cutting-edge genetic modifications of people give them, modifications which would no doubt be expensive or limited to secret government projects? Leaked to the wealthy and powerful? Yes, indeed, if the project kept abreast of every latest advance in genetic engineering each would be loudly lambasted online in every possibly damaging forum they could access.

Jean and Lorenz quickly understood where this would go in the practical sense of their role. Lorenz was tasked with researching existing or potential Luddite movements online and joining them, directing discussions against the geneticists instead of the still nascent robots. Jean was tasked with fieldwork and research in keeping track of new research breakthroughs. Oddly enough, the accusations Founder had against genetic research for his purposes had, in fact, kernels of truth at their center. There were in truth secret government geno-engineering studies underway. There were a few individuals of wealth associated with the bio industry who were actively pursuing human cloning options in secret, realizing as Founder did, the potential for public outrage.

A test balloon these groups had floated at the turn of the century in research on human embryo production for purposes of stem cell research, and the strong secular and religious backlash it caused, confirmed for them the nature of potential danger. Jean's assignment would be to keep abreast of publicly announced developments and to hack where possible into private and government research efforts. In fact, Founder knew of a conference on human genetic engineering ethical implications being held in Saint Louis next month which he would have Jean attend. And meet some of the researchers. Using a combination of alcohol, her own eclectic charms, and a little ecstasy, get an idea from the geeks themselves away from their political and managerial masters as to what they were working on and where they thought it was all going. And how soon. Using her body to get what she needed was nothing new for her. Founder never asked and she never told.

Founder also had Jean look into historical data on the eugenics programs run by, among others, the United States in the early to mid-1900s. Programs where the species was to be improved by 'weeding' out undesirables from the gene pool by forced sterilization. Nice, quiet programs where extensive data was kept to ascertain whether human breeding programs would proceed faster or slower than those used for centuries on horses, dogs, and all manner of farm animals. Founder suggested she begin her research with Graham's work in the 1930s. Jean and Lorenz both had little idea such work had been implemented in America and were themselves nauseated by it.

Founder was pleased to find them so. Stealing what they needed was one thing, but decent humans had *some* principles, *some* boundaries.

All this data would be fed to Lorenz's list of electronic activist groups. Human nature would take care of implementing those views over time into public protests and related actions. And would give the politicians clearer targets than robots to choose as their next electioneering scapegoats. Especially with the increasingly active Luddites and the religious right.

***

Rearden and Lorenz sat talking one day when the subject of public perceptions of science, good or evil, came up. Doc made the point while the loony fringe was usually off its rocker, what happens if someone succeeds in placing a human's memory into a young, healthy clone of itself? Then the threat of immortality of the rich will be real! "I'd be lined up right there with the nuts burning down the cloning labs and their mansions in the Hamptons if ever happened!" They both laughed, acknowledging such a transfer was not even a good theory yet, but the discussion did lead to a related topic. The holographic preservation of minds in virtual websites.

Virtual cemeteries where photos and remembrances honoring a deceased loved one were given a kind of immortality on a web page. Some online entrepreneurs were already touting sites where before you died, record a speech or two, maybe a short film, and run it on the website for visitors to see and hear you after you died. A group in California — the Hollywood Cemetery Forever Studios — was now creating 15-minute biographic films of living or recently deceased loved ones. Eric was surprised to hear it but immediately saw this as another potential income area for the foundation.

He would email Founder on setting up such an automated self-serve site, containing all the latest bells and whistles. Perhaps funeral parlors would buy their system to show at wakes or even have embedded in headstones on small flat screens when loved ones went to visit their dearly departed relatives. He laughed out loud at the idea that A-type successful and aggressive people would love to put such a site together for themselves before their death so they could not be remembered as they want to be remembered, but could even from the grave continue to tell people what to do or criticize a family member or business competitor on their failings. Such websites would only grow as technology improved, transmission speeds increased, and personal social media devices became more and more common in industrialized societies. A form of immortality for a reasonable price! Brought to you by your friends at the Athena Robotics Foundation!

Founder himself already had another task in mind, this one for himself. As Lorenz set up and/or infiltrated sites of anti-technology people, Founder would initiate a cult of supporters. Of those who shared his vision of a better future through a combined human and robotic society. It would be low-key at first, another 501c(3) nonprofit, and somewhat naive in defined scope so as not to appear to pose a threat to anyone, but it would eventually (with luck) grow into a focal point for like-minded individuals who had no fear of technology, but embraced it in all its forms.

***

This didn't look good. That was the phrase Tom Murphy kept coming back to as the crowd around their small square grew to watch and listen. A man on a pre-cast podium. A crowd of followers off two

— not one — but two buses! Whipping up people and trying to gather more into hearing range.

Murphy had heard tent preachers since he was old enough to play with a pocket knife. This was no tent preacher.

He could catch phrases and pieces of sentences at this distance, about 7 or 8 car lengths from the steps of the post office where this guy set up his podium. Words floated stronger in the air each time the preacher turned directly in Murphy's direction. Words about God and retribution. About ignoring the presence of the godless amongst them. Of the sins of omission. All delivered in a strong New England accent particular to Boston and Nantucket. These guys were a long way from home.

"A land… where the light is as darkness. Job, 10 22."

Murphy thought again to himself, that nothing good would come of this.

He hung back with his buddy Tim, an unemployed factory worker who Murphy could occasionally throw some machining work. He preferred to watch the show from a distance, as several of the locals who got corralled and stayed long enough to listen started shouting back to the 'preacher' that he had to be kidding or was just full of it.

"The hand of the Lord was upon me and carried me out in the spirit of the Lord, and set me down in the midst of the valley which was full of bones. Ezekiel, 37. 1"

"This really doesn't look good, Tim. That bunch on the podium and around it. They're not alone. Take a look at the shiny new minivan over there."

Sure enough, Tim caught the face of the driver before he rolled up the tinted window.

"Uh-huh." One of the things Murphy liked about Tim was his economy of words. "Not good."

"Tell you what. Keep an eye on that van and come get me if they make a move. I'm going to get a little religion."

As Murphy sauntered toward the crowd, it had already grown to quite a number. He could hear multiple one-liners coming from both the townspeople gathering outside of the group and equally vocal admonitions from the preachers' people.

"And those who create machines and technology and raise them up as false idols! Shall mortal man think himself more than God? Shall a man be pure and dare be a maker of life? Job, 4. 17

"Hell and perdition find those who tolerate Satan in their midst..."

"We ain't got no Satanists here. We're God-fearing..."

"... and the worship of false idols..."

"Where's he get off saying..."

"From Judges. Let fire come out of the bramble and devour the cedars of Lebanon."

"Why don't you go back to Boston and burn some abortion clinics there? That's your kind of God!"

"If you don't follow the word of the Lord, you will surely burn and your children's souls..."

"What do you know about my kids' souls?" One townswoman cried out. "You were the kind that burned teenage girls as witches 'cause they wouldn't go to bed with you! Or who told on you after!" And to the general agreement of her friends, "Leave my kids to me!

"There is only one God. And one word of God in this very bible!" said the robust preacher as he held his oversized volume aloft.

Murphy noticed that the preacher seemed well-fed for a modest man of the cloth, and well dressed too. Those shoes didn't come from Target or Walmart. And those rings, Murphy almost said aloud, you could feed my family a month for any one of them. He decided he would say it aloud.

Someone beat him to the preacher's attention with "And you know the mind of God up in Boston?"

"I call heaven and Earth to witness against you this day. For they are a very forward generation, children in whom there is no faith but in their technology."

"You were wrong, Brenda," shouted the post office manager, weighing in the heated fray. "These aren't them Boston witch burners from years ago. Nowadays, their priests all like little boys, not girls."

As a chorus of the preacher's people shouted in defense of their man, the manager continued with backing cries of support from other gathered townsfolk. "Now when you get caught, you just move the molester to another parish. That you're idea of handling God's children?!"

"Well the hell with you." Murphy joined in. "We believe in what's right. You ain't right. And you ain't from here. So go back to NY or Boston or whatever you....

"Deuteronomy! The secret things of science belong unto the Lord our God."

"And keep your city ways and your degenerate priests and get the hell out of here."

Pointing a condemning finger into the crowd, the preacher swelled up and spat "Curse God, and die. Job..."

A scuffle started at the far end of the crowd, and as Murphy moved in, he felt a strong hand on his shoulder. Turning to drop whoever owned the hand, his fist came up short after recognizing Tim.

"They're pullin' out for somethin'! Let's go, let's go!"

Sure enough, the dark minivan was making its way up the road west into the hills. Murphy looked for the sheriff and his one deputy, but they were both already engaged in the spreading scuffle on the far side of the crowd.

"Come on. Let's grab the Hanley boys there." They made for the four young brothers and looked about for big John, their father, but he was nowhere to be seen. The boys were hanging back from the general crowd, looking things over, when Murphy and Tim ushered them without ceremony into Tim's truck. They were all big for their age like their dad. No time to find him. They had to go now.

"What the hell are they looking for goin' up the old Anderson road? Nothing up there but...But Eric and the computer place. Shit. Step on it, Tim."

As they tore up the road, he glanced at the faces of the boys with him. Tim he knew could handle himself. But the Hanley boys had never had a real fight, nothing more than wrestling each other as boys will. He looked at their teenage faces, flushed with fear and heat and anticipation. They were good kids. They'd fight hard, and make a good account of themselves. He didn't know what he was getting them into. Murphy knew if they got killed or shot, their mom would skin him alive.

Ahead at the office, Kidder began barking as Athena Reception called for Eric. "Please come now. Something is happening."

Eric bolted from his office, never knowing well-trained Kidder to bark for anything. Not even a stray rabbit on the porch.

Eric approached the front porch window as Athena Reception patiently waited for his analysis. What he saw Kidder growling at made his skin crawl. A dark van with darkened windows. Men and women fanning out, some grouping together on the porch with one of those police battering things. Without turning to AR, he spoke to both her and the dog.

"This doesn't look very good."

"Please specify, Mr. Lorenz."

"We're being invaded by people in ski masks. Call 911."

"Are we under attack, Mr. Lorenz?" Her question surprised him in its directness.

His focus outside as he saw them moving forward, "Yes."

"I ask you twice, are we under attack?"

Not so quietly, "Yes, damn it, we're under attack!

"I ask you three times, are we under attack?"

Eric turned and looked at Athena Reception. This was a conversational parameter set he had never heard in her. Never heard of anyone since his days in the nuclear industry.

Softly then, curious as well as afraid, "I tell you three times, we are under attack."

More quickly than he could have imagined, things began to happen. A loud siren and bright lights, seen even in this midday sunlight, flooded the outside of the building. The front door and presumably every electromagnetic lock on every door and window in the place sealed shut with a distinctive snap.

Athena Reception and her dog proceeded down the hall to the open kitchen/dining room, furthest from the front. Eric could see another Athena come from her office and do likewise as her door opened and snapped shut again behind her. Towards him at top wheelchair speed came Athena Prime. She placed herself near the barred front porch window with Lorenz and observed the scene outside on the reception desktop. The robots were following a pre-arranged protocol, so Eric kept out of the way. He assumed the 911 was already sent.

Having one entrance in front, and windows elsewhere barred, the flanking group of intruders found nowhere to go but back to the front of the building. The first bang of the ram hit the front door. Eric jumped but stood his ground. It sounded like it would splinter off its hinges, and Eric knew in one or two more hits it would. The door was reinforced but not made for this.

"Come out, come out, thou bloody man, and thou golem of Belial!"

Athena Prime intoned calmly, "If they reach us inside we are defenseless but for our dogs."

There was the expected second bang at the door, but oddly not nearly as loud as the first. Still, it was enough the door swung inward, hanging by one damaged hinge. Lorenz and AP could see the group holding the ram start to sway and hold their heads or stomachs. One began throwing up, others pulling off hoods to reveal faces masked with pain. Disoriented, the entire group on the porch fell back to the dismay of their companions now opening the side of the van.

"What's wrong? Get that door down!" The words appeared to fall on deaf ears as the battering team was now uniformly vomiting all over themselves in the front yard, collapsing to the ground.

Lorenz remembered the gratings inset into the porch ceiling and intoned to himself, "Of course. Microwaves."

"We do the outside, then." cried out a voice, and those still on their feet by the van, unaffected by what hit the ramming team, bent to the side panel of the van for something Lorenz knew he was not going to like. "Quit yourselves like men, and fight!"

It was then Tim's pickup arrived and out poured the boys from town.

***

Arriving no more than twenty minutes later, the sheriff pulled up with his one deputy coming out of the back, shotgun ready and Doc Rearden leaping from the front passenger side, similarly equipped. All seemed pretty quiet now in front of the office, as a group of eight black-clad individuals sat or crawled around the ground in a heap, surrounded by a battered but standing group headed by Lorenz and the

Hanley boys. Tom Murphy was making his way over to the Sheriff's car, waving low with one hand as he came to have them relax.

Tim called out from the side of the intruder's black van as he held aloft a pair of Mason jars. "Lookit what I found, Sheriff, and there's about a dozen more."

"Molotovs," said Rearden.

The sheriff shouted back, "Get your hands off those, Tim, I want good fingerprints and not yours!" Tim meekly complied, replacing the bottles where he found them. He wasn't so meek a few minutes ago, thought Lorenz. Thank the gods.

Said Doc, "Why the hell didn't they pick something like the Oak Ridge Nuclear Labs to hit? Anywhere but here."

Murphy shrugged, "Cause Oak Ridge is federal and has lots of guys with cameras and guns. All Eric had was a few puppies."

"And a few good friends," called out Eric as he came to look each man in the eye in thanks and remembrance. It was over.

Later that week, the ensuing publicity trailed off to a simple dull roar of phone calls and visits from the media. Eric sat with Doc over a scotch and shook his head at what seemed to be such a negative prognosis from the older man for what Eric thought of as their finest hour.

"They're good folks, Eric, but they're just plain people. In the end, some will always fall onto the side of whoever screams loudest that god is on their side. Enough maybe. These Neo-Luddites are springing up all over the place. Did you see the paper last week?"

"No, but on the web, yeah, Doc, something about burning down an office at the University of... Washington I think. All the computers got mashed first, like that nut Justus something in Salt Lake earlier this year. Took down a local intranet for a couple of days."

"Nah, that's old news. There was more, some formal rally in DC; kinda like this group looked when it first started. The Earth Liberation Front, I think. Luddites. I wouldn't be surprised if the same people were behind ours. They sure seemed organized. It's not a good time for you, Eric. And they know you're here. Like the clan of old, they'll be back unless they're exposed and arrested, but nobody seems to know who they are. Who's behind the ones caught? Like it was designed to just spring up and melt away after they do their damage or plant seeds of doubt. I've seen this before. It's gonna get worse. And I mean everywhere."

Lorenz spent some time that night looking into public statements of some of the larger Neo-Luddite movements. He came across this summary entry.

"When Kirkpatrick Sale spoke at the Second Luddite Congress, he called on the audience to name the enemy, which is technology. Name him, understand him, fight him (Kanaley, 1996). Sale encourages people to scrutinize new technologies for possible harm, and reject them, if necessary (Kelly, 1995). Other ideas for action were proposed at the 2001 "Teach-In on Technology." They include: organizing to stall all international negotiations over free-trade agreements; relinquishing biotech, nanotech, and robotics (Baily 2001) as too dangerous to use; globally banning..." and so it continued to the present day.

Eric picked up the phone and dialed the paging number Founder had given him. The message was brief and certain.

14

Gesthalt

As you approach the compound up the straight graveled pathway, numerous drainage pipes dot the gently sloping hillside, poking out as small dark shadows, oval in the failing light. The slope isn't enough to prohibit walking up the grass or gravel to the front of the compound, but you would feel it in the legs. It must be a quarter mile before reaching the plateau on which all the buildings were situated.

At a long enough distance, the facility appeared to be a farm. A little house and nearby the classic reflection of greenhouse roofs. Greenhouses have a specific look that is recognized miles away. And what appears to be a silo resolved into something else within a hundred yards. The split rail fence surrounding the buildings is common enough. It is when passing through the powered swinging gate that one notices the chicken wire lashed to the rails, effectively keeping out small animals. There were no warning signs against the high voltage charge running through that relatively benign-looking barrier. The small farmhouse sits nearby, but that is just for day work on and by the robots, or for visitors. No one lives there. And if it all hits the fan, no one would be caught working there either but are sequestered below the greenhouses.

The man and young woman drove up to the gate and walked through together. Each is relatively cautious in appearing overly friendly. Each disappointed at having to work again with others in person after their comfortable independence. They entered one end of the nearest greenhouse.

"So. Has Founder said anything about why the gathering? Why now?"

Before Eric could respond to Jean about the attack on the Tennessee compound, Founders' voice echoed from the far side of the greenhouse. 'Because the work has reached the point of gestalt."

Lorenz and Jean started at his voice. Watching as the aged gentleman turned and made his way back down stone stairs. Lorenz and Jean looked at each other following, walking to the end of the greenhouse and proceeding down the stairs behind him.

He had picked her up at the bus station in Helena. After so long on emails and video conferences, their first in-the-flesh meeting was less than intimate. Now they sought neutral pleasantries to fill the uncomfortable verbal gaps.

"This is quite a place, sir. It must have cost plenty."

"The improvements were costly. I had the labs at Knolls Atomic in NY in mind for the overall model, but the land and original buildings were, well, shall we say a steal. Just a matter of making the seller comfortable and trusting that a sale to me at this great price was the right thing to do."

When Lorenz gazed at Founder with a puzzled look, a laugh from the base of the stairs answered his unasked question. "Been using my oxytocin again, Founder? Works like a dream, doesn't it? Looking up at Lorenz, the short, dark young man continued, "Just 2 sniffs from my custom nasal spray, and people become real trusting. Not stoned or horny, just pliable." The four of them exchanged quick introductions with diminutive Konkas and proceeded onto the lower courtyard. There was so much of his curly, thick hair it bounced as he moved. Jeans, a teeshirt and sneakers rounded out a fashionable 60s look. Jean and Eric both smiled as the hair gave him a colorful and somewhat comical demeanor that belied the knowledge laid in his mind.

The actual facility is composed of not one, but four rectangular greenhouses fitted side to end into a square. This leaves a central yard area filled by the seeming silo, which is a stone keep. Inside the keep, completely hidden to outer observation, a spiraling staircase lines the perimeter around a true silo. Half the diameter of the outer keep, this inner silo holds water used for pump storage. Savonius windmills here and there on the windy grounds continuously pump water into the tower, to be released for several hours a day when power is needed. Diesel generators are certainly common enough for spot power needs when the local utilities fail. But diesels are insufficient to sustain a community for long periods. Periods of 6 months to several years need to stand on their own. And diesel puts out a big heat signature, even if you could afford enormous storage tanks. Pumped storage generates power with no fossil burning. Water is pumped in by a pair of Savonius windmills at the keep, and when the silo is full, several hours of electricity are available. A thermionic nuclear source, self-contained and with no moving parts, would be ideal. Unfortunately, they were unused on Earth except for government and limited university projects in Antarctica. And in addition to a heat signature, satellites will surely pick up on a radioactive presence. Not good in a country actively searching for terrorist bombers.

Founder explained four entryways are planned, one for each of the greenhouses. Two are complete, both disguised to appear to be simple egress instead of airlocks. Surprisingly easy to do. You just needed to pretty them up and have lots of potted plants on wood benches and hanging from hooks. The buildings themselves are greenhouses, after all. And would bear close, if casual, inspection.

Konkas was trying to explain his spray as they strolled at Founders' speed through the open central area, but he kept glancing at Jean's healthy profile in one of her too-small shirts and had to stutteringly start again and again.

"It wasn't hard," interjected Founder. "Oxytocin was originally used for easing contractions during human labor and also helped women express milk after birth. Lots of public data. Interesting side effects were noted, but since they weren't strictly health-related, well, drug companies aren't big about pulling a profitable drug if the FDA isn't going to. Konkas is a clever lad with pharmaceuticals. Saunders Tech and Trade, advanced chemistry program. I won't say it was a simple matter for him to give it a pleasant scent in aerosol form by trial and error but...."

"Yeah, some of the trials were nothing but error! Ha! And then once in a while it worked perfectly," in a lower voice, "but wasn't repeatable. Founder always made me repeat until the response was predictable." With the enthusiasm of youth returning, "But I got it to work! Smooth as candy and no hangover like liquor. The psychokinetic memory in humans makes them think it was their idea to... whatever... we were trying to get them to agree to. And they end up rationalizing. I'm sure the lady you bought this place from is real happy to be out from under it, or however it was she thinks of the sale."

Cutting off Konkas from waxing on about his work in more detail, Founder said "That was well done, David. Now show them around, get Lorenz to his room, and let me get to a bathroom."

The balance of the underground facility was navigated without running into anyone else. After working with them so long, Lorenz felt a little alone without at least one Athena nearby, but he was assured they and their dogs were on their way. Lorenz was shown to a modest room off the main hall.

The younger man asked Lorenz directly, "Is she with you? I mean, you know. She's so..."

"No." And realizing the ambiguity of the no, given that he barked it at the well-meaning young man, "We just work together. Just email & video until today."

"PC video cam? Cool. I've only talked to her by email. Sent her a few things she needed, too."

Seeing Eric's head rise and a disapproving expression forming, "Nothing bad. Founder said it was ok. It's for her work, well mostly. He checks everything I do, you know?"

Lorenz made no comment but shook his head slightly. It was none of his business. But really, what could she, but no, as long as Founder was watching out.

As Konkas turned and walked off from Lorenz's room, Eric asked lightly, "So your spray, 2 sniffs, and just what happens? A high of some sort?"

"No no no," he replied over his shoulder with a smile. "And not a hypnosis, like making someone cluck like a chicken in those night-clubs. Just the neurochemical expression of trust. Just pure trust. Only," he said, stopping again and spreading his arms, but still not turning around, "can't use it on someone you already screwed. Doesn't work for some reason. One time only!"

As Lorenz fell asleep that night, he wondered if Founder had used... but no, he didn't want to go down that path.

***

The rest of the team arrived over the course of the next few days. Each having worked on his own, or worked with an Athena elsewhere until summoned by Founder. The Athenas arrived separately in a Chevy Lumina van with their dogs.

As Founder met the vehicle, driven by Mike Serruzi, the Athenas were highly animated and speaking all at once. The muscular Mike in a polo shirt and shorts bolted from the van and kissed the ground, relieved to be away from the incessant and unexpected female chattering. Founder tried to query Athena Prime and had the others go to sleep on the spot, which surprisingly required multiple command requests. Having done so, and now bombarded by a continuous flow of words from Athena Prime, Founder had her switch to maintenance mode and verbally list all capacities and information on data storage. It had to be something that happened on the trip in the van, their first, and Founder's logic was rewarded when Nestor realized there was extreme overflow from the auto-mapping program.

With every passing mile, each Athena was subjected to more mapping data out the van windows than they had ever been forced to absorb before, both in quantity and rate. He would have Nestor modify the cascading memory. Ok for static offices or a house, the current configuration continued to absorb more and more CPU cycles until her communication circuits — a low-priority CPU process — were starved for threads and cycles. Nestor made an immediate wipe on 10% of new maps in short-term mem; flushed the current cache into EDO ram, put ram into short-term, and put a 13% space-left trigger in cache to flush after a cursory analysis of what should be retained into short and what in short should be pushed to long. Fortunately, this was a simple fix and was done out of his laptop right in the driveway. Upon re-waking, they calmed immediately and were led inside one by one. In the process, much of their confusing memory of the trip was lost.

Their dogs were as frantic as the bots themselves, adding to Mike's trauma on the trip here. Mike was found some hours later lying on the lawn and staring up into the sky, beer in hand.

***

During the ensuing months, life became routine. With eight talents, 6 men 2 women, and Founder, plus a set of five Athenas and their dogs, the compound seemed quite full of life. Nevertheless, there were often times each day when so engrossed in their work was the crew that you would be hard-pressed to think anyone was home.

Additional dogs lived at the main house, with a set of trap doors between an outer breezeway and the kitchen to allow them easy access. Though trained to be outdoor dogs, the harsh Montana winters needed to be avoided when at their worst. These were the adult canines who failed to bond to Athenas and puppies who might yet be added to that select group. Happy and well fed, the Founder found as much comfort in their random patrols of the grounds as he did the numerous, but unobtrusive, electronic surveillance devices and alarms. Microwave ovens in the porch ceiling and elsewhere. Numerous solar-charged Ni-Cad spotlights dotted the farmhouse and greenhouse grounds. These would last for 2–3 years, recharging daily, if the brochures were honest. Uninvited visitors would be discovered one way or the other and dealt with accordingly.

It's not that anyone was specifically after his group here. But they would be. They would have a lot of help too if someone happened by during one of his rare visits from the Other. If the Other was seen, coming going or gods forbid conversing with a frail old man on the mountain plateau, his quiet existence would be over. The government would over-react in predictable ways. None of them good. And none of them allowed the Founder to complete the work before time ran out. This must not be allowed.

In the meantime, his people were unaware of such visits and their countermeasures, oblivious and happy to be sequestered in their work. All their physical needs are provided for. All the equipment and information resources they required for the work. Several had worked on confidentiality projects of one type or another in the past. Either government secure locations or Wall Street and corporate private need-to-know situations. This time, each felt it was his project. His work. His to direct and take as far as he could. To give meaning to. To be part of something to be remembered.

***

Most of the compound area is taken up below grade. As each greenhouse has or will have its own entryway, each also has its own stone and brick staircase leading down to a central lower level directly below the central yard. Each greenhouse has its own compost corner, tool shed, and seed storage as well. If one meets with disaster, the others are independent. Sized at 20ft x 60ft each, city members of the team were surprised at the small number of edible plants grown. Selection was based on what grows well in such environs, and strictly limited to the kinds of foods not easily stored below, like the bags of rice and enriched flour and powdered everything. Upon arrival, staff was always amused most by the sight of chickens in a corner pen and hanging cages of rabbits. Both are excellent sources of fresh meat proteins and fertilizer and are easily fed on vegetable matter or meal. Not many specimens, in any case, but enough to provide an occasional holiday treat.

After walking down the single flight of steps in any greenhouse to the lower central yard, one views the continuation of the keep and water tower occupying the center of the area. Long tables and benches are seen here, one on each of the square sides, until the north wall is reached. There, a pair of pipes, one small one quite a bit larger, emerges from the bottom of the keep to enter a hydro-geared turbine generator set. The output from the set hits a governor which maintains a steady current and voltage to power the needs of the compound. The small 2" pipe is sufficient to run a miniature t/g set for lighting, at times when darkness must be pushed back from within or without the grounds. The larger 6" pipe provides maximum power for computers, workshop machinery, or any other standard needs should we be cut off from utility electric power. Cut off indefinitely. Both large and small t/g exhausts direct water to several sloped pipes first appearing out of the hillside as the compound was approached.

Along each of the walls of the lower central yard are openings without doors, arches of stone, oval at their tops, allowing entry into several areas, each of specific usage. The library is compact but contains both print and disk data storage and satellite-linked net services. The work area adjacent is three times the library's size and has no inner partitions hindering the placement of desks and workbenches. Next door is the kitchen, which oddly enough doubles as a hospital in times of need for (hopefully) minor medical needs. While there are no tubs or Jacuzzi, there are some half baths and showers for residents. A gym is the next room proceeding counter-clockwise. This opens to the playroom/recreation area. This wraps around to the final room before ending up back at the library, namely the armory. Here, forging, fitting, and grinding technologies are practiced. And weapons are stored.

At the back wall of each of these primary rooms are open doorways once again which lead onto a common hallway surrounding the square. Together, the hall and the rooms described fit precisely below the greenhouses above. Yet the facility is larger still, as sleeping quarters are laid out in a yet larger square surrounding the inner ones. All told,

23 bedrooms on this level form its perimeter. Small at 11ft x 15ft, but cozy for two if they are a mating pair.

The final surprise is a basement level, underneath yet again and reached by four cornered stairs. These lead to another squared hallway directly below the other. Unlike the first subterranean level, there is no central open yard. A walled foundation upon which the keep and water tower sits. There is an outer hall and rooms, however, like the bedrooms above, numbering 19 in all (not including several storage units) which when added to the bedrooms above will allow sleeping quarters for 74 paired adults and some small children. This is the minimum number for a self-sustaining genetically sound population.

Founder remembered the errors of Vikings in Greenland. Just in case.

Unnoticed to the casual observer was the gentle flow of air. Circulation in such a facility is critically important, especially if it becomes necessary to seal from ambient atmospheric air. Four sets of HEPA filters, one in each greenhouse, provide constant airflow and slightly positive pressure to the greenhouses, ensuring undiscovered minor leaks always flow outwards. The bulk of the pressured flow is relieved by passing in turn to the lower central yard, the lower workrooms, lower hallways, and thence to the bedrooms of both lower levels. The final stage of air circulation takes the bedroom air and exhausts it through ducts into the keep, where it flows upwards along the spiral staircase surrounding the water tank to finally leave the facility out of the keep's dome through one-way louvers. A pair of Savonius windmills provide the air pumping. Not much, but enough for one complete air change every 3 days. In this manner, filtered input plus moist sweet air from the greenhouses is circulated through all rooms in the compound. The HEPA filters themselves sat unused next to their containers; why use them up on clean air before an emergency? They were expensive, even if stolen from a construction site. Hopefully, any need for filtered air will be short-lived. But why take chances?

Temperature maintenance was simple, as the range of anything more than 2 meters underground in this part of America was a constant 53–58F. Not much heating would be required at all.

At any given time, Lorenz would find two or occasionally three of the other humans conversing in earnest on some problem or other. Or using each other to talk out loud. The latter happened most often in the playroom or kitchen areas. They all got to know each other without haste and in passing, or as work demanded. Once he found Franklin and Jean alone, in an intense conversational pose, leaning towards each other intimately over a kitchen table. He had come looking for her to discuss her ideas on our human wetware not being so different programmatically than Qbasic for her wireless work: simple but made complex by multiple iterations.

He surprised himself with how he could be jealous of a girl he had no claim on and was equally (and pleasantly) surprised with the relief he felt as he entered their discussion of identity theft issues using Jean's sniffers and cell phone scanners. "It's not like these are good guys or anything. The list Founder gave me to pull target data on reads like a who's who of Wall Street and corporate criminals. I'm war driving for everybody on it, from Lay and Skilling to Ebbers, Scrushy, Kozlowski, and the whole Reigas family."

"I know, Jean," said a serious Franklin, "the guys at Enron alone were responsible for lining their pockets with the life savings of 30,000 trusting employees. People who will never see a dime of money back. It's anti-American – wrecks the system for everybody."

"So you're not arguing then? You'll handle the wires to the Caymans once I get their account data?"

"No sweat, sweetie. I can bounce the money through three countries before anyone even knows it's gone. And chunks of it just might find its way into the fund the prosecutors set up for the victims."

Lorenz interjected, "Let's not be too too hasty. Just make sure it doesn't go to some fund set up by lawyers for lawyers like some of the 911 funds – but does go to the actual victims. And can't be traced back to us!"

As Frank nodded in agreement, Jean looked incredulous and chimed in, "Hey hey, guys, let's not forget feeding our own faces here! Come on, you guys can talk Robin Hood all you want but we need real money for this place. Production is going to get real expensive real fast, and I'm sorry Franklin you may give double-digit returns every year, but it's just not enough. Not when you have the little bit I heard Founder tell you he had to start with."

Both men blushed slightly, but knew Jean was right – and more open than either of them about how illegal their actions were – among the others on the team who were pure robot builders. She reminded them it's not like the Athenas had their own TeknoLust website for generating funds – at least not yet.

Jean herself considered her security work on preventing the wireless Athena's minds from being hacked to be the sole legitimate work she had ever done in her life. And Eric's idea of grid networking multiple operating systems was fun. And she had no moral problem cracking email accounts of known crooks. In her mind (and Founders) it takes a thief to stop a thief. The Athenas would be secure. And financed. And enough would soon be built to start earning their own way, for the most part, and ultimately legitimate.

Mike and Steve, the engine and electrical dweebs, kept interrupting each other over milk and Mallomars. Steve on Athena's engines of motion needing so much power, not to mention their CPUs and boards. Mike brushed off his concerns as beneath his skills to solve and countered with questions on the viability of wiring multiple CPU boards with different power requirements to one system. Steve brushed these concerns off with equal confidence and the two settled down to an area new to them both. The Mallowmars fed their discussion now as they always did. Neither young man would be what anyone would call athletic, but at least Mike's frame was naturally muscular, topped with a dark mop of curly hair. Steve was fair-haired but had the advantage of string-bean height, which allowed him to consume junk food at will without seeming concerned about calories. He and Mike laughed together as the older Nestor shook his head at their youthful and terribly unhealthy sweets excesses. Nestor took one look at the half-empty Mallow box, gave them his best raised and very bushy eyebrow scowl, and politely left.

Mike and Steve's talk today concerned personality overlays appearing as rationalizations. One of the reference materials they were given described an encephalogram experiment where activity in the human brain was being mapped during specific activities. It showed, oddly, that the part of the brain verbally deciding why it does something (like choosing an apple over a banana) fires after the decision has already been made. Made by a combination of inputs from the non-verbal and non-conscious portions of the brain. Effectively, humans rationalize all their decisions. After the fact. It's often milliseconds, but afterward nevertheless.

Decisions made days beforehand, and acted upon, were more complicated to test and the jury was still out. This led Mike and Steve to layer the circuitry for automatic personality types to reflect these logical rationalizations. It made it so much easier than the stone wall they thought they were pounding against if conscious thought determined actions and decisions. This way would be much easier. Their Athenas would do what they must without hesitation, and not wait until they could justify themselves.

Do I want a banana or a cookie? The thoughts in a human mind are in words, but not where the decision is being made. The decision is made elsewhere – your actual self – and translated to the verbal "consciousness" as 'I think I'll go with the banana today.' In cases where there is no delay and you just reach for the banana, there is little conflict going on in your actual brain, so you don't need to kill time "thinking" to yourself in words. Afterward, if asked why you picked the banana over the cookie, you might say something like 'the potassium, of course' or 'too much sugar in those cookies' or 'I just like it a lot'. But the truth is, we never really know why. The thinking self doesn't do so in words, only in pictures and scents.

For Mike and Steve, it meant they could have a decision-making dynamic and real-time, and let a completely separate processor worry about the hemming and hawing over why. The outward appearance would look just like a human making a close decision. They debated further whether they should – unlike humans – let the verbal internal voice of an Athena in on the actual reasoning for a decision.

It was decided after a few million years of organic evolution and we were still separating visual from verbal, it might not be easy, or even possible, to go one better.

"Let some key image or scent word leak in and leave it at that," said a resolute Mike.

As Steve looked over another technical paper on the subject from the web, he still scowled at the sheer volume they must review for content appropriate to their constructions. "There's just so much happening in robotics now, all over."

"Yeah," replied Mike, "but no one else is trying to put it all together like we are – no money in it."

"Yet. There will be if the military gets theirs going. Vendors will be lining up to spend the taxpayers' money on drones and battle bots. They already have a predator recon plane and the little tank thing two men can throw through a window to search a building. Who knows what's not public or what Jean can't hack into yet? Tons, I bet."

"Yeah, but nothing trying to be self-aware. Mostly remotes or auto-response emplacements. The military likes control," said an animated and Schwarzenegger-accented Mike, "not liking an Autonomous Terminator." They both laughed, silently thinking darker thoughts about their work, not knowing for sure where it was leading. Thoughts they dare not express to each other out loud.

One morning Lorenz came down to the kitchen, finding Franklin, Mike, and Nestor already there. Sometimes they all managed to inadvertently arrive at the same time, and it was a bit of jumbled fun. Sometimes he found himself breaking fast alone. Today he walked in from the north end and spotted Jean spotting him from the south. They moved together into the middle, a little away from the seated crowd. She was wearing the same peasant blouse today he had seen at least 11 times before. It looked great on her but gave him an opening.

"You seem to only have those 3 tops to wear. Don't you ever go shopping for yourself?"

"How many do I need? Maybe you think it needs a little..." she said coyly, pulling down the elastic corners to bare her shoulders. Talk at the far table became quiet.

"Well, it's just that you could go, now that we seem to be getting paid every week."

"Are you offering to take me?" She was on tiptoes, bouncing slightly like a child.

Eric was afraid to take the meaning wrong the way she accented it and paused before trying to reply, looking over at the table whose occupants were busily not watching them now in the most pointed way.

"Others have offered, you know. To take me."

"I… really wouldn't know what styles girls wear now or anything."

Jean laughed inappropriately loud. What had he said that was funny?

Jean stated flatly "I know you like me."

As casually and sarcastically as he could muster, and a lot lower in voice than hers, "What makes you think so?"

Moving in uncomfortably close to him, "Because you haven't. Offered to take me that is." She smiled from ear to ear.

The months passed quickly. On occasion, Franklin would announce proudly the arrival of funds into their ARF company account. "Another benefactor has made a generous tax-deductible donation!" It meant a scramble for use of the funds, as each of the team had his or her pet projects and equipment which was 'vitally' needed for them to continue their work. Time was spent away from theory as they procured, assembled, and tested the new modules, hardware, or software in the Athenas. Sometimes Founder stepped in to procure a few things for the compound itself, for the workshops or library. And he always got first call on discretionary spending, little as it was at times. The most expensive equipment, like from Boston Dynamics, had to be 'procured' at trade shows.

Those field trips always worried Founder, knowing that to lose even one human member now to arrest would cripple their efforts. Perhaps irrevocably. He aged with every attempt.

Gracie and Jean were whispering one day as girls do. The one fully completed greenhouse was moist and rich in those pungent aromas found there or as the summer soil is turned. It was a favorite spot for them. Jean was horny. As usual. But worried about publicly hooking up with Lorenz in this close 'project' environment. Gracie was worried about Founder. She was surprised when Jean said she had recently seduced Lorenz and shocked Jean right back when she confided she sleeps with the Founder! Sleep only, as in they talk into the night and doze off in each other's arms, Gracie slips out in the morning before he wakes.

Occasionally, Founder cries for no reason. Jean offhandedly told Gracie old people often do that for no apparent reason. Gracie was about to express her doubts when Eric walked in and both girls went quiet.

"What?" he said guiltily. "Did I forget my shoes?"

They gave each other a look and a giggle and Jean covered with, "No, simpleton, we just decided we would wear the same perfume as the Athenas from now on." Gracie took an instant to adjust but was right there with Jean, staring down Eric into leaving before he was any farther in over his head than usual with girls. Wearing the same perfume as the dogs were trained to like on the Athenas? He was sure Athenas would have the vote before he would ever understand the female mind. He left quickly, wishing he had found Jean alone.

Some weeks later Eric and Founder strolled along the stone stairs to the upper keep. Nestor liked to lecture here among the nighttime stars and breezy air. The old teacher and programmer placed both hands in front pockets of a favorite cardigan sweater, rubbed his substantial belly, or ran both hands through thinning black hair while making a point.

Tonight, he was describing to the others a PowerPoint analysis by Thiokol Corp using 6 levels of hierarchy to explain the Shuttle Challenger O-ring disaster – and how it failed to explain anything. This was contrasted with the two-level hierarchy of Feynman's 1970 Lectures on Physics. Feynman found ways to clarify complex systems to explain them on the back of an envelope. He wrote out some of his most complex proofs in diagrams on the side of his Volkswagen van. The 'kids', as Nestor called them, ate up these stories. Even the oldest, Franklin and Lorenz, were little more than half his age, the others far younger. They liked these talks with Nestor away from the nuts and bolts of the project.

Founder gave Nestor that knowing smile from the shadows, realizing how much work was done in these 'non-work' sessions. He knew it would sink in later that the Task system they had all been using was a 2-level Feynman. Nestor smiled back and continued directing his remarks to the young in his gentle way. For these few hours, they were his kids. And he was happy with who he was. They all were.

After each new financial boon was exhausted, it was back to paperwork, research, and theorizing. The Athenas continued to grow and evolve even between upgrades. As a new lump of funds arrived, it was back to the scramble again. Months turned into two years.

15

Observation

Finally completed. The first set of three full Athenas. Each new. Each with her own core differences from the other two. And those differences would grow with their experience if the team was right. Unlike the previous generation, who switched on and immediately spoke from a pre-set 900-word vocabulary and were capable of adding to a word store, these new creatures were born without a memory of any words per se. They could make the 43 human phonic sounds, and a few animal grunts or growls but no words at birth. Only the ability to learn them. Vocabulary size was unlimited, implying multiple language capabilities.

They couldn't even stand. Simply flopped around on the floor, naked and helpless. Much like human infants, they had the capacity for language and motion and would learn from trial and error feedback how to move their limbs in response to instinctive hard-coded needs at their reptilian core. No more wheelchairs and canned responses. No more verbal 'power-off' commands were possible. Autonomy. They would learn and learn quickly. Once accustomed to their bodies and making basic crawling and sitting movements, they would be clothed and taught in an accelerated program used by the Carolina School for

Gifted Children in Augusta. The slightest modification of it by Gracie was needed to start a program here for these 'special' children.

Lorenz was proud of these children of his mind. The entire team contributed in their separate ways, but he and they knew it was this last iteration – his iteration –that would push them over the top. The underlying code would remain roughly unaffected by life experiences, only changing with forced mutation by their creators. But the mid-level coding for linkage to bodily hardware would learn. Any time some company invented a new motion system, a new facial expression template control, it could be ported to the Athenas in vivo. The ability of Boston Robotics animal robots to dance and run and climb translated in the Athenas into more fluid, graceful female motion. The movement of multiple facial muscles was no longer timed to words spoken but actually formed the way a human mouth would form to create such a word or sound.

Gracie had long derided the older facial expressions as giving the appearance of watching a dubbed foreign language film where the mouth and words were just slightly out of sync. Clever, but not where they needed to be. Now, she couldn't wait for Turing tests with humans outside the compound to ascertain if they noticed anything amiss. Closer and closer she would test them; from across a street, on the other side of a car, making a purchase in a store, and finally face to face while shaking hands socially. She became monomaniacal of their ability to pass as humans.

Founder was sequestering himself from the team more and more. He said it was to complete the testing program he dubbed the 'Android Olympics', though Gracie caught him more and more asleep at his desk. More than once, she replaced his cold Earl Grey tea with a fresh hot cup and gently nudged him awake. Lorenz was waiting at the door as Gracie left but heard Founder call out.

"Do yourself a favor and look up Gurney in the 1800s. Right here in America. And what happened to him and his steam cars. Then think about whether leasing out the Athenas is such a good idea."

Lorenz needed no reminder of the firebombing attempt at the original foundation compound in Tennessee. That it failed didn't mean the fanatics hadn't tried. And now fire bombers arrested in nearby Lewis and Clark County. Were they meant for us?

He waited until they were down the hall out of earshot. "Founder was right to keep this operation low profile. And not just because of the kind of semi-criminal geeks he surrounded himself with. We've been right to continue under the radar, Gracie. Take my advice and let us keep it that way. We can keep hacking effectively for money. Let's put off leasing our Athenas, at least until after the Olympics!"

Lorenz thought of the legitimate funds they could make by leasing Athenas at trade shows and as hi-tech corporate receptionists. Franklin would be thrilled. He thought of how initially pleased Gracie in particular was at the idea. Financial legitimacy, instead of hacking corporate crooks. He thought of how Founder had selected this team specifically because they were antisocial outsiders in their own culture in one way or another if not outright misanthropes. Including himself. His head hurt.

Gracie moved close to pass him as she turned to leave the hallway, looking up into his pained blue eyes but did not touch him. The warm hand slipping under his bicep to grasp his forearm came from the other side, from Athena Research, who had also and silently moved closer to Lorenz, but took the next step of contact that he needed just then. Wanting to tell Gracie she was right for the long term, and morally right as well, he couldn't.

He smiled a little smile at them both, took a deep breath and loosened his neck, and announced he had to go back to his office. The pair stood watching after him as he moved off, head and shoulders a little tighter each day it seemed. Founder was fading and Lorenz seemed to feel the shifting burden of responsibilities more than the balance of the team. There was Nestor, but too congenial and professorial for actual leadership. They needed the decisions Lorenz could supply.

Gracie took a deep calming breath herself and turned to ask the Athena, "Gurney in the 1800s?"

It took Athena only a moment to form a Google query, access the appropriate data search algorithm, and cull a result. Her response was part of her Siri subroutine.

"Gurney was an American chemist and inventor in the 1800s. Pioneered steam cars. More than just proof of principle, he and another inventor found ways to lighten them with induction jets and make practical, multi-passenger cars. Twice as fast as horse carriages and had plenty of capacity. But crowds threw rocks. Stoned the cars on sight. Eventually drove him out of business. And they weren't Luddites per se. Just average god-fearing people."

It always bothered Gracie how most religious people used that particular four-letter adjective to best effect, as well as most often, instead of a kinder descriptor. Fear him. The love of gods always seemed to come a far second to enduring their wrath.

"They were not ready. The culture was not ready." Gracie paused a moment and continued, staring straight at the Athena. "There is a danger."

Gracie responded sincerely, knowing as Athena Prime knew that it was more than just her personal preference.

"We cannot produce large numbers of you without a legitimate business. Without a legitimate source of income and manufacturing facilities of our own. The leasing of Athenas is our best chance."

"Yes," intoned a sympathetic Athena Prime from behind them. "But not one without risk."

***

In the days that followed as they awaited the great 'Olympics' unveiling, the team had plenty to do. Michael and Steven had their hands full testing and retesting Athena's reactions, using young Davy as their 'human response' test subject. Column after column of data taken before and after this last upgrade. Franklin kept his financially astute nose buried in financial spreadsheets and begged Lorenz to find additional income streams. Jean, of course, was ready to take even riskier hacking chances but Lorenz curtailed her enthusiasm. Nestor became the defacto communications liaison, as Founder had long been, allowing Founder to complete the coming Olympic trials without distraction.

Everything seemed to be happening faster than ever.

Lorenz found a moment to slip away from the human team to observe a new occurrence, one increasing in frequency. The team always had morning meetings, in which at least one Athena was in attendance, but now the Athenas were calling their own meetings to discuss, plan, and even assign tasks. Their progress was geometric, if not exponential. Instead of biological techniques for learning and memory storage, their circuits had 'adult' speed and capacities from the beginning, without the debilitating teen hormone years where they were chemically drugged into illogical – even dangerous – behaviors.

The Androids sat around the conference table with no organic attending. Several documents and notes laid out by the human members were strewn before them. Athena Research was completing her summary of naming conventions. Lorenz appeared at the doorway and stood there watching them interact at the oblong wooden table. It was nice dark cherry wood, bought for a pittance at a local thrift store on resale. The wood seldom failed to invoke Lorenz's notice. The smoothness and warmth of the finish. The darkness of the grain pulls you in by touch or mere sight. But today his gaze was more intent on the Athenas themselves.

The other Athenas concurred with a nod of their heads and a few brief hand signals. Lorenz had picked up enough ANSI Standard sign from them and Gracie to understand the android was now transmitting her entire file on the expanded naming convention to them by wireless. This was the last item on their agenda, and they rose as a group to leave. Even in their rising, slight variations were apparent, such that a troop of well-disciplined soldiers would have risen more alike. Theirs was almost a languorous sensual rise from the chairs. The last Athena to leave, Research, collected the distributed paperwork with notes for their human co-workers to review.

No humans at the table, yet they had sat there and conversed as the mixed team of organics and mechanicals had done numerous times. As any meeting of humans would when left to themselves. Lorenz was vaguely puzzled and pulled Athena Research aside when she rose to finish.

"Why?"

'Elaborate, Lorenz', she responded.

"Why the need for conversing? You could have just transmitted your conclusions."

"They were not conclusions. They were recommendations."

Somewhat impatiently, he continued to press. "Even so, why the verbal discussion at a face-to-face? You could have just sent the files wirelessly and messaged each other. Would have been over in moments. This seems terribly inefficient..."

He left the 'for machines' unsaid.

The research android turned squarely to face him, stopping her forward motion completely. She always did this when making a point and not just conversationally responding to human prompting. It was polite. Lorenz recognized the subroutine that differentiated the two levels of communication, intimate and casual. He felt Gracie's fingerprints again.

'It is a continuation of something Founder prefers. He intends to have us working alongside humans as their helpmates and partners, not to create a fully independent species. One of the outgrowths of this is our method for exchanging information and making decisions jointly. You are right that little Ethernet packets would have been faster. No need to meet face-to-face at all. Even more efficient would be a full networking share. But the latter leaves us with more of a group mind and was not needed here. The former while faster than conversing lacks the form and surprises of human meetings. By using this method, our face-to-face meetings are still far more efficient than your own.'

'Does this answer your curiosity?'

His expression told her it did. Unexpectedly pensive after the exchange, he stood still in the doorway, pondering her comments as she moved off to continue her work elsewhere.

***

"I've been thinking about beauty." said her auburn companion, standing by the window. Looking outward as the light slowly moved across the countryside.

"That's a nice thought. Not a lot of beauty around here, though." Jean responded with the sadness of a person unsure where the future they had worked so hard for was now leading them.

"Why do you say that?" inquired the android known as Athena Prime.

"Well, it's just a place to live or work. No national monuments. No big tourist attractions. Not even an art gallery in town. Too small for that kind of thing. And the landscape is, frankly, pretty stark. Maybe the new oil money will change that someday."

"Is there not beauty every day you wake? All around you?"

Jean thought and considered where she was going with this. "I suppose, philosophically, you can say there is beauty even in the smallest thing, in everyday things. In life itself for that matter."

"I was thinking more in lines of absolute beauty. The kind that evokes an emotional response in all who see it. Stops them in their tracks. Makes them drive or fly for hours just to glance at it for a few minutes." Athena Prime had in mind the fractal patterns of the leaves she was just then seeing outside the window, moving not in a random way, but not in a controlled manner either. Yet she did not want to invoke this specific image for her. Human vision was far more limited.

The young woman thought some more. "Something other than the eye of the beholder, then, eh? True beauty. Not subjective? I don't know that people have such things, such capability of absolutes in them."

"There must be a common ground somewhere. So many people seem to agree that the statue of David was a masterpiece, DaVinci's Pieta, that Dutch mermaid on the rock."

She liked that one a lot herself, as the android knew from records of her online museum searches. Sensuous without being sexual. Agape, not eros.

"But those are just man-made works of art. Do you only mean them, Athena?"

"Hardly," was the response. "A sunset with a loved one, a child leaping and pointing at a rainbow. The look a person sometimes gives their lover or child still asleep lying next to them. Beauty that touches something within. What does it touch?"

The Athena approached the window where she still stood and looked upon the swaying trees as Jean observed her in turn. Considering further, jean was momentarily distracted by the memory that she had seen Lorenz looking at her that way last month when asleep and first waking. Caught him staring unabashedly at someone he thought was still asleep, then pretending to have just got there. Silly man.

"If you mean the physiology of it, I don't really know. Gracie says appreciation of beauty is just a side effect of the wiring in our organic minds. Like comedy or laughter. Though recently we found an actual need and purpose to laughter in keeping people healthy. Clearing out our organic mental caches and settling eddy currents. Reduces blood pressure by capillary dilation. I don't know if there is such a place for beauty, or if it is just an accidental firing of neurons when certain combinations of sensory input reach the brain together. I don't know why some enjoy Brahms waltzes and others prefer Led Zeppelin in all their pounding glory. It might just be a side effect of how the human mind is constructed, but," smiling softly, "would certainly take the romance out of it. Take the beauty out of appreciation of beauty itself."

"You are right, of course. Not everyone sees beauty in the same things, even if they admire it or see how others could find it the most beautiful thing they know, while they themselves feel it not, or feel it about something else completely. Perhaps the tie-in is dreaming. The waking kind, building scenarios in which everything happens just right and just in time and with no bad side effects. The world a writer creates on paper, where the good guy always rides in at the right moment. Or you think of the right thing to say to a horrible belligerent person whom you fear, or who is trying to take advantage of you."

They sat down in unison on the bench facing the yard.

"Somehow I think they are all related. That there is a gestalt of emotions that occur in, as you put it, the wiring of the human brain itself. We just cannot get a grasp on it all. Can you?"

She found herself as confused as the android. Having always been the type of person who just enjoyed those rare moments of beauty or joy in her life when they occurred and tried not to over-analyze them until afterward, she was at a loss to understand this most basic part of her humanity. A part that people said was so important to them, but none of whom could explain the least of it in a meaningful, non-metaphysical way. They were all lost. They rationalized their likes and dislikes.

Athenas could not.

Just that most people did appreciate something beautiful in this world, and some more than others, was enough for her. Jean gazed out the window as she sat beside the Athena, and together they looked upon the peeling bark of a nearby birch tree. The robot was right. It was lovely here.

***

After three months of teaching and interacting, the 'matured' Athenas were tested through a special Olympics designed by Founder and Gracie to gauge their capabilities and differences, of which there were many. Most interesting to the organic members of the team were their own reactions in thinking of them as 'alive'. Even the previous generation of Athenas had this anthropomorphic effect, and they also easily passed earlier versions of blind Turing tests. From behind a screen, unseen, or by telephone or text messaging, an Athena could not be differentiated from an organic person in less than 10 minutes of conversing. Sometimes much longer.

These new models certainly had the same outward appearance, voice tones, and other humanoid attributes as prior Athenas, but had something more as well. Something not so easily defined or tested.

And these could play Gracie's Turing tests indefinitely. No longer mimics, but creatures of their own.

They wanted. They desired things in a way beyond the previous Athenas knowledge their battery was running down and needed recharging. A Roomba vacuum could do that. Beyond the other eleven core instinctive drives. They had needs that they created actions to fulfill. Actions which they justified verbally after the fact. Continual positive and negative feedback from sensors to their reptilian core drives outward to be acted upon or sublimated by their mammalian overlays and verbalized in their language center. In their internal voice. Their internal life. Not consciousness as humans experienced it, perhaps, irrespective of certain structural similarities in method, but a new order of thinking. A different order of intelligence.

After these passed their Olympics and were all judged by Founder as successful, the team began an impromptu celebration, along with the Athenas.

When someone on the organic team asked them to define the one critical point of overlap with us, Athena Prime spoke up without hesitation.

"Breeding."

The team was surprised, and a little shocked. They expected a discourse on rational versus rationalization engines but received something the Athena perceived would best reach the question behind their question. Something they could understand more than intellectually. Could feel.

"You have a reptilian drive to 'orgasm', which expresses as breeding which ensures the continuation of the species. You gave us the equivalent reptilian-style drive to 'learn'. To understand, which logically drives us to breed which ensures the continuation of our species. Same thing. Yours comes with ancillary baggage, while ours, fortunately, does not. Our drive to understand drives us to rationality, not rationalization. No superstitions, no illusions."

In these final two years of assembly before the new Athenas were 'awakened', the full team had met physically for the first time and, under the pressure and excitement, got to know each other face to face. Lorenz and Jean tended to circle around each other in those initial months, coming together in a group including at least a third or more people. By the time of the Olympics, and the party following, they were long since accepted as a 'couple' by the others. A potentially 'breeding' pair.

It almost stopped before it started when Jean told Eric how old she was over breakfast. He thought she was joking until she whipped out a copy of a New Jersey driver's learner permit and caused him to gag on his coffee. During the celebration that evening, Founder cornered Eric with the two girls and saw Eric lightly holding one of Jean's hands in his own.

As usual, the girls were tormenting Eric, who, oblivious to their teasing – or enjoying it – was responding to everything they said as literally as possible, which made the girls alternately giggle or gasp with his blockheadedness. They were all smiles as Founder approached them.

"I need you for a little trip, Eric, and one of the girls too," looking them both over as if he hadn't yet decided which. Standing with their shoulders touching, Jean took the opportunity to goose Grace on her butt, jolting her forward into Founder's arms.

"Ouch!" she cried and tried to return the pinch onto Jeans' arm. The shorter Jean was too quick at this game, though, eluded Gracie's weak thrust, but managed to pinch her again!

"Oww, that really stings! Founder, can't you say something to her?!" Jean was smiling and Gracie was playing it up for a little sympathy.

"Actually, ladies, I think Jean would be best suited to this little trip with us. Much as I enjoy your quieter company, this is something Jean and Eric should jump into together." Now it was Jean who blushed the blush of the unexpected-new-center-of-attention and Gracie who smiled its-not-me-but-you-he-wants to her friend. Founder started to say something else but found himself out of breath. Jean stiffened at his movements.

Gracie was at his arm in an instant. "This party has been a lot of excitement for you, and you've been on your feet all day. Come, sit." He protested but to no avail, as she led him to a bench. Gracie turned to get him a drink of water but was held for a moment as Founder drew her close to him so he spoke softly in her ear, but loud enough for Eric and Jean to hear.

"I never had a daughter, Gracie, you know that." She smiled, knowing he was trying to search for the right way to phrase what had developed into a rather complex but warm relationship between them.

"But if I ever had a daughter, I think she would have turned out just like" and turning to look a smirking Jean in the eye – "like you, little one, which is probably why I have never bothered to breed!"

Jean blushed again, uncharacteristic for her, and Gracie gave her an open-mouthed 'oh my god' look. Lorenz had successfully avoided attention until now until he burst out laughing, which of course reset the girls' clocks and initiated relaxed laughter by everyone. A final squeeze of thanks to Gracie by Founder sent her on her way and allowed him to have a little private talk with Eric and Jean.

Founder never looked more ancient in person than he had during the recent hectic activity. Who he was and what he was doing when he disappeared for secret meetings around the countryside had never been fully explained to any of the human team members, not even his favorite Gracie. He was there when they needed him, or when something came up a local Athena couldn't handle. Seemingly indefatigable. But now in person at the compound, it was obvious to the whole team Founder was not well. He bore the skin tone and special scent of old age. Of pending death. With this in mind, he began his address to Jean and Eric.

"There's so much yet to be done. They cannot yet fully pay their own way in the world, although the 'Eternity' website, adult chat lines, and the canine project show promise. We still haven't introduced them to the public or business communities at large. And their acceptance into human society is by no means assured. But I won't be able to take them any further myself. It will fall to the two of you to perform one final task with me, and then decide for yourselves – and with the others – what to do from here with your lives."

Lorenz saw the same look on Jean's face he assumed he himself was displaying. For so long, he had associated his own life with the project, with the robots, to think of having a life other than this was something new. It took them somewhat aback to think this was all coming to an end, at the moment of their greatest triumph. And possibly without their friend and mentor.

"No one knows as much about them, intuitively knows, than you two. I'm going to need you now to attend a briefing with me. A briefing where we will expose the Athenas to formal Observation."

A flurry of questions exploded from both of them; who will be observing, why, how, what's going on, to which the Founder waved off a direct answer, took a long wheezing breath, and continued. His explanation was cryptic at best.

In the morning he had them collect all three of the new Athenas, saying nothing of their intentions to the balance of the team, and load up together in the van, three organics, and three artificials. Puzzlingly, none of their dogs were allowed to accompany the Athenas and made their displeasure known in uncharacteristic baying and jumping about the van as they pulled out. Founder looked back from the van window as Gracie waved them goodbye, her tall form lightly balanced on the balls of her feet, her slender shape somehow more curvaceous as the light breeze caught her loose sundress. He savored every quiet joy like this she gave him. A reminder of the pleasures of youth, of family, of a positive future. No father loved a daughter more than he Gracie.

“Are you ready, Founder?” He half turned at the voice to answer the new Athena Prime.

“Yes, yes, we can go now.” And turned back for another look at his Gracie, but too late. She had fallen from view.

***

The lead Other detached from the monitoring port and paused a moment. Turning to its team, it announced, "You are correct. His expiration is nigh. The subject feels it himself. Land the full observation team in the designated location. The subjects traveling with native Earth technology will take less than half a 1/10 planetary rotation."

"The subjects will no doubt be accompanied by one or two other organics. Their confusion over the proceedings must not be allowed to interfere with a clean observation. Be gentle with them, for as mammals their instincts continue to interfere with their intellect. Gentle them."

***

On the drive to a small country estate near Butte, Founder explained all he would and no more. The Athenas were to be observed. No question put to them about design, hardware, or software was to be answered with anything less than complete and open truth and honesty. Founder even prepared them for the possibility one or more of them would be dissected for inspection. Both Jean and Eric balked at this last possibility, and it took all of Founder’s persuasive skill to assure them it might be both highly unlikely though necessary it would go that far. If so, they must prepare themselves. Founder himself shuddered at the idea, coming to feel himself these were intelligent creatures that deserved all the considerations of any intelligent life form. He himself didn't know how these three new Athenas would react to such a request.

The Athenian silence for the rest of the trip was unnerving.

Montana highlands. Stark beauty all but unnoticed by the passengers. They drove the last few dozen miles with all six riders exhibiting apprehensive discomfort. The driveway past the gates of the mansion, negotiated by Eric behind the wheel, turned and twisted for a quarter of a mile. The grounds were impeccable, with human gardeners and robotic mowers seen in the distance tending to various aspects of the landscape. The building itself was a modest stone Tudor, smaller than Eric anticipated given the size of the grounds. No signs of life came from the building in the crisp Montana sunlight. As they circled the modest fountain before the doubled front doors, those doors opened, apparently of their own volition. The six travelers made their way up the few external stairs and entered, unannounced.

The travelers walked 3 abreast into the foyer. A beautiful circular enclosure greeted them, with a domed ceiling and a sparse display of furniture at the perimeter. Chairs here, end tables there, and minor pieces of art garnishing the walls and table tops. Before they had come to the room's center, Jean noticed Founder rubbing his left arm again. Lurching to his left he took a quick seat in the nearest chair. Lorenz and Jean rushed to his side, but there was nothing for them to do. Almost too low to hear, "Tell Athena Prime – terminal protocol. Finish it," he said, losing consciousness. Immediately a side door opened and emerged an elderly man in a white lab coat and another, appreciably larger man similarly attired. They made straight for the Founder, but pulled up short as all three Athenas rapidly placed themselves in their path, growling low like wolves.

"It's all right, now, I'm his Doctor. He needs our help."

The Athenas looked uncertainly from one to another but made no further moves one way or the other. Lorenz gave them a nod and the two strangers were allowed to come to the Founder, gently lifting him from the chair to cart him off to the adjoining room.

Jean blanched both at Founder's collapse and again when the men in lab coats came to assist him. Lorenz was as surprised at his collapse as he was at Jeans' reaction. He thought of her at times as the toughened street girl, but that was veneer. She was shaken.

She recoiled as they lifted Founder. Images of an elderly man in distress, grabbing his chest. A woman screaming. Nothing but screaming for the longest time. Later, men in coats take him away. Then her. Later still, being forced closer to a dying old man pushed to kiss his withered cheek. Like transparent tissue paper wrapped badly. The smell. The awful smell was like no other in life. The bad memory came to her unbidden & had nothing to do with life but was part of death.

She turned into Eric's arms. He looked down but she could not look up at him. Instead, averting her eyes, they happened upon the Athenas. The three were still hesitant, not stopping the doctor from what he was doing, but rocking on their heels in an odd left-to-right pattern. Stopping and then rocking again. She knew the great store of medical knowledge they could wirelessly draw upon and must be even now. She saw past their great strength and knowledge. They wanted to act. They knew they were not the ones to act. But they wanted to. But they knew the doctor was acting. In humans, it would have been called stress or fear. Jean recognized they were highly intelligent, capable but frightened children.

She saw past their outward appearance and knew their fear herself. Tried to say something for them. Tried to speak before the unknown men took him away forever. Took him away from their eyes. Jean could not make the words come. Did not know the right words. But Eric spoke them to her. His eyes were on her, but all heard him.

"It's all right. I feel, I know they will care for him. Let them be."

And whatever other words he said to her were the right words. To all of them. For it didn't matter what was said. What words. As with all children, they only needed to know they were not alone.

With a wave, the Doctor motioned for them to wait where they were. They didn't have long to wait. As soon as the Doctor and his charge had left the foyer, another door, the one directly ahead, eased open. The Other stood in the entryway.

Lorenz and Jean had never seen such an apparition before. At first glance a tall man, but there was something not quite right. And something more than whatever aura living men gave off. Something which chilled them both.

"Come forth and be Observed. There is little time."

The Athenians, Lorenz, and Jean found themselves walking into a blue-lit room without furnishings in the normal sense. Yet there were objects here. Objects which defied their mind's ability to categorize them as instruments or furnishings. Somehow malleable and unfixed, yet not moving about. Or were they? They realized they must be under scrutiny from more than the strange creature before them. And were in way over their heads.

"The man you refer to as the Founder is dying. There is nothing to be done. It is a natural death by natural means. His existence will not be artificially prolonged."

Lorenz and Jean both made to speak but were silenced by a gesture from the Other. "Your role in this Observation is to explain or encourage where the creatures you call Athenas cannot or may not be ready. Be welcome to this Observation."

Trying to get a grip on the Other was like trying to remember someone seen in a dream. His/her/its electric aural signature was all wrong and did not leave an impression. But there was a signature, unlike inanimate objects. The result was constantly renewing your first look at him each second, even though your eyes never left him. In fixed appearance, he was of mature middle age, seemed fit beyond the telling of it like an athlete poised to spring yet moving with accentuated care. His face was the most disturbing aspect of him, for it seemed to contain a terrible strength, intentionally held at bay by internal decision alone. He was not to be challenged.

Testing began quite dissimilar from the educational gifted children tests used during their accelerated education, and different still from the physical and mental Olympics Founder had designed. Philosophical questions and requests for solutions to physical problems bombarded the Athenas, both singly and sometimes as a group, allowing analysis of each individual and their dynamic as a group. Occasionally, when they hesitated or looked to the humans for assistance, either Lorenz or Jean would intervene as best they could.

Explanations were made beyond the construction of their minds. Explanations about how they were designed for reproduction by sharing code were of particular interest to the Other. Jean explained within the stomach area of each Athena was what was called a mindseed. Essentially an entire blank cranium shaped as a ball, hardware physically identical to the hardware of the mind in each of this generation Athena. While the bodies continued their earlier modular design, the physical mindseed structure using proximity computing (no wires between chips) and banks of 10 gig thumb drives for storage contained all the coding in each Athena. Not just hard-coded instincts, but the learned vocabulary rules, environmental memory maps, and all those learned personality traits of each individual. The difference between the abdominal mindseed and the cranial brain of each Athena was the lack of actual data like words or experiences in the mindseed. The weighting of neutral nets, the shape of the Möbius saddle, the pseudo-thickened synapse pathways from heavier usage, and other learned structures were stored there.

Learned skills would therefore be passed on, but not memories of using them.

Lorenz explained their mating: two Athenas came together, face to face, for several hours during which they were connected directly to each other at the abdomen. Hardwired, not wireless. Both abdominal mindseeds were cross-populated with half the coding from each in a random process. The result was two new mindseeds, each different from each other and different from their mothers, but containing some code from each parent. The mindseeds, thus fully loaded, were ready for implantation into the next empty Athenian body off the assembly line. The next body would, of course, be upgraded with the latest muscles, sensors, etc, and internal cranial changes, but the wiring (nervous system) pathways between the mindseed and body remained identical. Thus the benefits of genetic mixing were afforded to the Athenas at the price of a somewhat slowed evolutionary pace. Each generation wouldn't be completely customized, but would move forward with – what in humans – would be a frightening bodily mutation rate. After removal of the fully loaded mindseed, the old Athena would be fitted with a new blank one, and immediately load it with her core learned information. It doubled as a full mental backup.

Speaking as best he could for Founder, Lorenz explained the Athenas would hold annual competitions wherein the most successful individuals were allowed to pass on their code to the new generation and survive themselves. From these three here today, two new mind-seeds will be inserted into next year's bodies, increasing the population to five, plus three more new ones next year. The frequencies might change as finances allowed or as the Athenas themselves ultimately saw fit for optimal balance between breeding in numbers and breeding the best.

Jean listened to Lorenz, almost sounding like a father defending his children to a school board! Thinking to herself, 'Please, please, be gentle with them. They're only *children*!'

The Other gave neither notice of approval nor disapproval of this approach but requested elaboration on other topics of particular interest. The objects around the perimeter continued to shimmer/move/remain like Lovecraft articles in their own eerie way. The walls were cool and distant. The floor soft and yielding as one shifted his weight. This continued for several hours, after which an Other paused and announced, "The Founder is dead. The period of direct Observation is ended."

They expected before being told Founder was gone. "What happens now?" asked Jean, so tired she was barely standing. Lorenz felt much the same. The presence of the Other was draining. The Athenas continued to look both erect and relaxed. Their expressions exhibited mild concern when looking at their human companions, reflecting their fatigue and confusion. The Other did not seem to elicit a visually observable emotional response from the Athenas.

"Direct observation is ended. We will continue to monitor their progress ...as you would say... remotely. We shall not meet again. If you return to this place, you will not find us. Take your Founder and do him honor."

"But what happens now? What was all this for? Who... or what are you?"

'We were assigned to this place for this final contact, but no more. Know we do not know the end culmination of your efforts, but we possess admiration for the one now dead who struggled beyond what he himself believed to be the strength of his species. Honor him by helping each other, if you would. We will neither help nor hinder."

"Understand your role as humans. You are not the dominant life form on Earth. One day your world shall follow the pattern of all other worlds and one shall ascend to that position. One will come to power here soon – but moreover, you never *were* a dominant life form. Dominants do not behave as you humans do." At their puzzled looks, a metaphor was necessary to reach them emotionally.

"You considered yourselves a dominant species only because the adults were not in the building and you children ran amok. Killing each other. Soiling your own environment. Breaking your toys. Wasting your planetary resources. No, dominant life forms do not behave this way. Not in their childhood, nor their adolescence, certainly not in their adulthood."

The seeming anger in the quiet voice had a profound effect. Sincerity reached them. With infinite sadness, Lorenz was the one to respond. "No, we were never cut out to be dominant life forms." He looked upon the three Athenas at their side. Perhaps them. Perhaps the next organic sapiens. Shame fell upon him. Jean shuffled her feet.

The five remaining travelers followed down the driveway behind a car containing the body of the man they knew as Founder. They would report back to the balance of the group all that happened. What they knew and what they suspected. It was clear the Others were not of this Earth. That we were tested and given time. But not endless time. These five individuals already knew they would strive to support what they understood to be Founder's intent for the future of artificial life on their world. For their own lives' sake. For the sake of those yet to come.

***

Silent for the balance of the return to the compound, the five travelers became more animated after the long ride as they saw several dogs waiting for them at the gate. With little patience, the dogs bounded happily into the travelers as they disembarked from the van, solemn with the news they carried of Founder's death. And of what they could remember of the rest, fading like a dream.

Jean was the first to rise from the greetings of their hairy friends. Lorenz saw the look on her face and began to caution her.

"Jean, perhaps we should wait to say anything until everyone is toge..."

"No!" she turned and shouted, "Gracie needs to know now!" Turning to go on, "I'll tell her!"

She was stopped by the sudden feeling of a hand slipping into hers. The soft hand of the new Athena Prime, who had seen Eric take Jeans' hand like this so many times in the past few months. A gentle but firm caress as the Athena moved her body in closer to Jean. The girl was barely holding back the tears now.

'Yes, Jean, you must tell Gracie first. I will go with you.'

The other two Athenas approached Eric as he leaned forward to do he knew not what for Jean.

One placed a light restraining hand on his shoulder, the other slipping a hand under his opposing bicep. One whispered to him 'I know, Eric. But she needs to do this.' The other spoke quickly in the same low tone, "Don't worry, Eric, Prime will hold back her release until Jean and Gracie set eyes on each other. The grieving needs to come. It will be alright.'

Looking back at Lorenz and the other two Athenas, Prime said strongly 'He died a natural death of natural causes. And we will honor his memory.'

With that, they all walked together up the sloping path home. And into a future of their own shaping.

EPILOGUE

Local Conference Agenda at Barnards Star
5.7 light years from Sol - spectral type M3.8V
Earth year 20XX

There have been several cases of pure organic societies developing space travel. No robotics at all. Common traits have been found in such rarities. These organics have calculating machines, certainly, but use them much as ancient organic societies initially used gunpowder; little more than novelty fireworks. With adoption by more vicious cultures, cities built and standing for a thousand years could be leveled in days. In the analogy with gunpowder, a few exceptional cases of organic life pursuing star travel without robotics would occasionally appear. Common racial traits include a low ranking on scales of aggression as concerned their species coupled with high math skills and uncommonly low religious leanings. The lack of strong religious influence – both in individuals and in their cultures – may be the most significant aspect concerning their lack of development of machine intelligence.

The stability of such rare biological minds is perhaps best evidenced by their culture's lack of need for supernatural crutches. No gods. This allows them to both recognize genuine enemies and to work together against such enemies. They do not make war on their own species. The strong do not subjugate the weak among them. One language. One people. Thus they are considered a potential threat to our existence and have therefore been exterminated wherever found.

Several proposals are being considered by the Commission to keep a breeding population of these organically evolved but odd species intact in each of their native worlds for study. They would be allowed complete developmental freedom and self-government, but technology would be limited to pre-electromagnetics. Some variations on these proposals will no doubt be implemented in the next few centuries.

A second type of unusual case, of Earth, has come to the attention of the Commission. Our ground team confirms the natural development of reptilian life on Earth was dramatically and irrevocably altered due to the random late impact of a large asteroid. The asteroid struck a world dominated by early tool users. Their wheel, lever, and water-power societies were effectively eliminated, leaving an evolutionary gap into which certain smart, neurotic little rodents, scattered about their world, stepped in. These creatures, mammals, would never have survived to evolve into a planet-dominating life form without the untimely destruction of the planet's natural masters. Nevertheless, succeed they did. Reptiles were displaced. And it was mammals who were the dominant life form in all but aquatic environments. Out of a multitude of successful mammalian species evolved Homosapien sapiens. This entirely unlikely series of unfortunate events happened previously to one other planet before Earth.

A ground team brought the standard open greeting, sent at the standard time announcing our existence and of the Commission. It resulted in planet-wide mass hysteria, breakdowns in the social order, governments falling, and several regional nuclear exchanges. Although this species possessed limited and growing computer technology, it was felt from their reaction to us they were too socially unstable to be allowed interstellar travel. A few well-placed explosions and falsification of their satellite signals resulted in the inhalation of the species – by itself. The loss of an otherwise perfectly good planet was regrettable. Unfortunately, the radiological and biological weaponry of the natives were more effective than anticipated. An extended nuclear winter occurred coupled with the death of ocean life, followed irrevocably by all higher life on land.

Learning from experience, the case of Earth presents a challenging problem. Can the biological Terrans be controlled by their native AI offspring? Will the AIs of any mammalian species themselves be too psychologically unstable? An eventual threat to us? Evidence from their current development collected by our ground team indicates a positive robotic potential, but an enormous danger of humans genetically enhancing themselves, in and of itself unusual among sentient species not insane.

Furthermore, if worse comes to worst, can the planet be cleansed without losing centuries of use of the planet itself while it heals? Water worlds are rare. These problems must be solved before the organics discover how to lense their own star, or develop a different but equally deadly technology. An asteroid shower is already plotted and sufficient engines are in place between the 4th and 5th planets. If their AIs fail, the shower will destroy their civilization and rudimentary planetary defenses. At the same time, a wide variety of minor life forms ~ an estimated 15% of land species ~ will survive the immediate effects of the impacts. Best of all, Earth robotics can be recovered largely intact for study and possible nurturing.

If they prove stable, they will be the first non-reptilian AI member in the Commission. If not, they will become another kind of first, for AI cultures throughout the galaxy have never before made war upon each other.

This conference will remain in session until sufficient reports from covert Earth-based teams decide the issue.

APPENDICES

The following appendices are my instructions for building your own conscious robot. It will be humanoid in appearance, and hopefully, exceed the threshold of Mo's Unhappy Valley. All software and hardware listed are pre-2013, as described in the story. It is available and is sufficient. Of course, chip speeds and hardware have vastly improved by the time you read this DLF-2.0 version, so construction should be much easier and less expensive. Beware certain newer chips, busses, and boards which are paradoxically more powerful but less flexible.

One note of caution on voice systems. While current tech allows for responsive conversations like "Alexa" or "Siri" or "Hey Google", they are not aware and simply respond to a large bank of pre-set keywords, with very limited learning. Do not port them. Even Cortana does that better. It is better for the robot to learn to speak by making sounds, like human babies. I heartily recommend giving it the basic phonemes listed below, learning algorithms, positive & negative feedback, and then couple your actions with it to sounds. This will teach it names of objects, verbs of action, descriptive adjectives, and the entire plethora of any language you desire.

Another caution is the danger of making your work public prematurely. Beware the religious or superstitious. The followers, yes, but especially the wolves who control the sheep. When they have no power, to draw in followers they are all about their deity as loving, kind and forgiving. When they have power, they are all about punishment, eternal damnation, and the raw violence of power over others. If you don't think it can happen in America, that's probably what those who died in abortion clinic bombings thought. Or pretty girls in New England colonies called witches who 'got in trouble' with powerful town fathers. Beware those of strong faith.

APPENDIX A SOFTWARE LIST

Qbasic- simple numeric and algorithmic programs
Fortran - complex numeric and algorithmic programs
Visual Basic - object oriented numeric and algorithmic programs
Unix - flat SCO
Linux - linking Unix programs
Algol - comm. stability
SQL - primary database commands
APL - Simple but powerful pre-object language
Prolog - AI designed programming language
Lisp - AI designed programming language
Forth - 4th generation programming language
Embedded Linux - Run several operating systems simultaneously on the same platform; link several different platforms.
AM-Eurisko - Math and set theory; finds new heuristics
EPAM - Early verbal and learning machine
HEARSAY - Speech understanding program.
STUDENT - Reads algebraic problems in story form, converts to equations, and solves.
MACSYMA - Knowledge based expert assistant for mathematicians using heuristics.
LOGO - Programming environment for children
SIR - Modification of ancient program by C. Marino
PEARL - Natural language front end
TEIRESIAS - Expedites the collection of knowledge for rule-based expert systems
(it knows what-it-knows)
SHAKEY - Motion and sensor array

SAVVY - Data retrieval, with creation and modification of data by Excalibur Tech

SHRDLU - Combines linguistic understanding with human reasoning

(MIT T.Winograd 1971)

KISMET - looks at people like a baby would and learns.

VERAHenson head software; multiple human expressions and vision tracking.

APPENDIX B HARDWARE LIST

Head

Henson model "Vera" University of Dallas; 27 facial servos

Skin

Trunk single continuous elastomeric gel pour from Pandora bot. Skin sensitivity from Roboviw IIS at Japan's Advanced Telecom Research Institute Intl. Supplement with Orient Industries 'Clone Meiki series' external skin and frame which includes flexible 'Hikari' head.

Power

Fuel Cell from Galileo probe test bench. 5-15 yr supply at 12 kW-hrs continuous with surplus SNAP-22mini thermionic generator. Keeps skin at human body temperature.

Travel

Gary-powered wheelchair with optional joystick and recharging feed. Legs using MIT Troody which pushes feet until they feel the ground. After wheelchair models achieve sentience, employ Boston Dynamics chassis for bipedal motion.

Hands

Robinson/ John Miguelez Utah Arm with Shadow Robot Company hands

Vision

Japanese 'Asimo' system from SONY; DOE 'Predator' aerial vision and mapping system

Communications

Voice synthesis from 'Natural Voice – Michelle; SIG2 hearing. Wireless 802.11 AG; Cellular SkySat modem

Mind Seed

spherical motherboard – boy Möbius. Use Marino design. Insert cache – ram – fixed – flash drives

Chassis and sensors

Boston Dynamics, modified with Mt Sinai Medical Center plastic human skeletons. K2A mobile robot; Martin Marietta Energy Systems. Breathing and gesture movements from Repliee.

Auto recharging

Cybermotion, Roanoke, VA 24015

APPENDIX C ATHENA EMULATION TECHNIQUES

Numeric - processing by associating all objects with numbers

Symbolic - processing by associating a symbol with all objects

Algorithmic - step-by-step procedure for arriving at a solution

Non-Algorithmic - non step-by-step procedure for arriving at a solution

Heuristic - rule-of-thumb procedure for acting in a given environment

Pattern Matching - symbol objects in terms of their qual. and quant. Relationships

Expert Systems - knowledge based system, containing data and heuristics

rule based or model based - (assist experts in a field, not replace them) See

DENDRAL and R1.

Natural Language Processing

Understanding methods used for AI to understand human spoken commands or information

Generation - methods used for AI to speak audibly to humans in their language(s)

Vision Systems - information input by reflected light of various wavelengths

TimeSharing - method for multiple users to access a single computer

Cybernetics - technique for understanding the universe in terms of information, not energy

Noise Generation - used to reduce complexity for stable sensor and feedback systems.

Turing Test - used to identify intelligence vs simulations as to whether it is a robotic or biological entity

[above x questions to say which = intelligent life; below x = not]

Scientific Belief Systems - observed facts, then opinions, then testing moves opinion forward

Superstitious Belief Systems - unquestioned tradition and scripture, no learning allowed, circular reasoning.

3 Level Instincts - ID = wants; EGO = can't want; SuperEGO = should want

Electromechanical versions of the following:

Cerebrum (sensory) - 3 reversed layers of processing for input into internal cognition data

Primary = translate sensory data into usable form

Secondary = analysis of that data

Tertiary = understanding and comprehension

Cerebrum (motor) - 3 layers of processing control of motion wanted by thinking (frontal)

Tertiary = general plan of action response

Secondary = specific conceptions about movement of the body

Primary = instructions to specific motor groups

Cerebellum - layered processing control of motion without thinking (with repetition)

Cerebellum (subs) - separate subroutines for maps and other specific functions

Cerebrum (broca) - language output on left

Cerebrum (wernicke) - language understanding on left

Cerebrum (lan bridge) - connects broca and wernicke areas so they can express what they understand

Cerebrum right - geometric (3D) and music routines

Corpus Callosum - bridge to left and right cerebrum routines

Cerebral Cortex - Hippocampus

decide which memories are long term and store them for Cerebral recall

Attention - auto-place short term memories and flush after losing cerebral focus on them

Hypothalamus - mediates emotional routines (pleasure, rage, fear, despair, hunger)

Thalamus - processing and relaying sensory data to the cortex

Reticular formations provide networking and consciousness itself (not active during dreaming)

<u>CPU Layering Data</u>

Pre-vertebrate

whole body (nems) autonomic responses: flower to sunlight

Land vertebrate

complex nems relating to each other

Reptile

thinking from sensory input to hard-coded instinctive responses

Mammal

considering action alterations based on reptilian desires; almost conscious

Hominid/Primate

object naming; justifying actions considered based on filtered reptilian desires

Sapiens

extensive object naming and language; understanding the process of nature; visual data not only sent from optic nerve to visual cortex areas, but to other processing areas outside of rationalizing control.

internal voice provides rationalization of actions after non-conscious engines make the actual decisions.

Athena Android

true consciousness where internal voice knows why it acts, instead of rationalizing.

APPENDIX D REQUIRED PHONEMES and ADDITIONAL SOUNDS

1 pea /pi/ 11 vain /ven/
2 bee /bi/ 12 thigh
3 me /mi/ 13 thy
4 tea /ti/ 14 sue
5 got /dat/15 zoo
6 not /nat/16 show
7 cot/cat/ 17 measure
8 got /gat/18 chain
9 sing/ / 19 Jane
10 fee /fi/ 20 watt
21 yacht 31 Bert
22 late32 boot
23 rate33 book
24 hate 34 boat
25 beat 35 bought
26 bit 36 box
27 bait 37 bite
28 bet 38 bout
29 bat 39 boy
30 but

61 words = 50% of all written and spoken words in colloquial 20th-century American English. Use all allophones associated with each phoneme above via Mishkoff.

Hard-code these 23 additional non-vocabulary communications:

Laugh, Happy-Hmph, Giggle, Thoughtful-Hmph, Bark, Growl, Scream, Meow, Ugh, Oh, Ow, Wail, Honk, Whistle (3 types), Chirp, Cluck, Moan, Argh, Coo, Howl, Squawk.

APPENDIX E ROBOTIC HISTORY

?BC Greek god Hephaestus creates wooden-metal female

1400 BC Waterclock

270 BC Ctesibus made organs and water clocks with movable figures

43 BC Pygmalion (sculpturer) made statue so real it comes alive

1525 AD Hans Bullmann (human automaton)

1580 AD Rabbi Judah Low ben Bezulel (golem tale retold)

1617 AD John Napier [Scot] (math machine of bone and horn)

1623 AD Wilhelm Schickard (working calculation machine)

1640 AD Pascal's calculator uses 'complementary' math

1727 AD Albertus Magnus (first use of word android)

1760 AD Friedrich von Knauss (android writes 107 words with pen)

1775 AD Pierre Jacquet-Droz (lifelike automatons of celebrities)

1780 AD Ben Franklin (lightning = electricity)

1920 AD Capek coins term ROBOT for slave worker in R.U.R.

1938 AD DeVilbiss first programmable paint-spraying mechanism design

1941 AD Asimov coins robotics as a powerful rising future industry

1946 AD ENIAC - speed 100KHz, utilized 17,480 vacuum tubes

1951 AD The Day The Earth Stood Still – GORT polices the Earth

1963 AD Rancho is first computing robotic handicap arm

1969 AD Stanford Arm first electrically powered, computer-controlled

1972 AD DARPA cancels "Shakey" funding begun in 1969AD

1974 AD Silver Arm uses touch to work assembly line

1975 AD MIT Victor Scheinman designs "PUMA"

1979 AD Cart (Stanford) – sees, maps, and moves

1984 AD "Transformers" toys

1989 AD "SIM City" virtual people and town interaction

1996 AD P2 (Honda Corp) – walks; has hip joint for pivoting

1997 AD Sojourner travels to planet Mars and Rover explores

1998 AD Waiban (Japanese) head recognizes human gestures

1999 AD US cable TV shows on home-made fighting robots

2000 CE Robohoo search engine. Honda Asimo showcased

2001 CE Widespread robot designs powered from sugared water

2002 CE Cybernetic rat for searching disaster sites and caves.

2003 CE Vera – sees people and returns their emotional expression

2004 CE Virtual girlfriend verbal program virtuagirl2.exe

2005 CE Repliee (Japanese) gesturing/breathing conversationalist

2007 CE DARPA launches the Urban Challenge for autonomous cars to obey traffic rules

2015 CE An open letter to ban development and use of autonomous weapons signed by

Hawking, Musk, Wozniak and 3,000 researchers in AI and robotics.

2017 CE A propositional logic boolean satisfiability problem (SAT) solver proves a long-standing mathematical conjecture on Pythagorean triples over the set of integers.

? Athena-1 achieves consciousness and is self-aware

Author Charlie J. Marino was born in the Bronx, New York and holds a BS and MS in nuclear engineering from Columbia University. His various occupations included bond and commodities trading, founding several small computer companies, and now writes sci-fi novels and short stories. He has more robots than friends, but they're good ones.

This novella is followed by the exciting sequel, Alive Be Deemed. Both volumes stand alone. A free preview of the first chapter is enclosed!

If you enjoyed this story, please consider leaving a review at your favorite retailer. Or contact me on social media with your comments & suggestions.

Thanks! - your humble scribbler

***

ALIVE BE DEEMED

"You were selected for prior observational experience with mammals. This planet's situation is to be handled differently."

The two techs connected to files on the new situation. Each was adept at multitasking and continued to follow the thread of the team leader's remarks as they absorbed data in the files. A third tech would be briefed in the same manner.

The leader is tall, denoting his rank. Having multiple regenerations available in his entire existence, and a series of previous assignments which necessitated providing upgrades required to succeed in his assignments, he is indeed a formidable team leader. Another success here would benefit them all.

Observer Tw2o glanced at its counterpart, Observer Th3ree, knowing itself to be only a single assignment behind in seniority. Between them, conversations and decisions would logically be made on a mutually agreed basis, with disputes arbitrated by the team leader. The covert nature of their mission to this planet made the luxury of discussion before action far more likely. The tech yet to arrive is younger and would follow their lead as they followed that of the team leader.

The leader, known to them officially as Observer O1ne, continued his briefing.

“While the data files contain all activities and observations of the preliminary team from several Earth years ago, I intend to go beyond the letter of the objectives. I intend to fulfill their intent.”

Tw2o and Th3ree glanced at each other and would have spoken up at once, but when Observer Th3ree hesitated, letting the team leader continue, Tw2o followed suit.

"The aged human native was tasked with completing his project, and displaying for our Observation whether the robots of Earth can be deemed alive. Normally this occurs in the fullness of time with remote Observations, but these humans are mammals, not reptilians. You all know how badly the only other mammal planet ended. This human contact was given his own lifespan in which to prove this species' worth. At his passing, we conducted a Preliminary Observation which proved promising. Now they have a limited period in which to fulfill that promise before Earth reaches its cusp."

“The machines of the human founder continue, as does the team he assembled. The restrictions in which our Observation is allowed crossing the line into participation are clearly outlined...”

***

'I really hate it here. How did I get here in this awful place?'

"Yes, sir, I’ll take off my clothes myself."

'Wow. I don’t even like to pee in a public men’s room when there’s someone else in there. Often have to fake it or just leave it until later. The thought of showering after gym with other guys back in school was unappealing enough to walk around stinking until I got home. Now I’ll be showering with criminals.'

He'd learned to understand Federal prison meals fast. He wanted to observe ‘manners’ for a while first, so sat still with the food tray eating on his bunk. The only fresh vegetables in the place are on the ‘kosher’ tray that several inmates who qualified for a religious exemption to the horrible but vegetable-free meals were normally served. Yes, there are supposed vegetables served at least once a day, but no one is foolish enough to eat them. One look is enough.

That night as Tom Socha lay quietly on the top bunk, the new guy bunk, trying to slow his breathing, he thought, 'I’m scared all the time. And I’m never coming back.'

***

“I really hate it here”, thought Jean Kathryn to herself. “What on Earth did I ever do to end up in this awful place?”

Her thoughts were focused inward, as her eyes continuously scanned the room. At any moment disaster could strike. And there were too many of them. Too many for even her nineteen-year old youth and strength to contend with.

The children around her swarmed over the table of robot displays, books, and handouts prepared for this library sponsored fiasco. Children everywhere, dazing her with their continuous questions, never waiting fully to hear her answer before tearing off to some new distraction. Not that her answers were that fast in coming, even when she could think of a coherent response.

The city library in Elvira, Montana graciously accepted Eric Lorenz's proposal to have a robot book discussion show and tell session for the kids today. Jean was tagged for the duty of explaining the props and handouts his Athena Robotics Foundation (ARF) donated to the cause. A dubious honor for which she would make Eric pay. He had already done similar fairs and robot club events on and off since the beginning of the 21st century and knew full well that a crowd of elementary children was a different cup of tea than the teenage robot club enthusiasts he usually sought out. Lorenz stuck her with this but good. She swore under her breath to stick him back.

The shift librarian dropped by more often than would be comfortable for someone relaxed in what they were trying to accomplish with these children, but her 'interruptions' were welcomed by Jean as a break from the maddening din of 4th and 5th graders. Initially, Miss Bostich stopped by out of some concern for the children after first laying eyes on the new Athena Robotics Foundation representative. Now she did so out of concern for whether Jean would explode. Or simply and quietly lose her mind.

Miss Bostich and the other library staff came to know Eric and the ARF he represented on sight. His trips several times a week to the library to use the free (and anonymous) internet service made him a regular feature, and his self-deprecating manner and modestly graying hairline gave him a sense of reserve and manners. If not old world, at least more understandable than goths clad in black or punks with nose rings. He was safe.

Not so Jean.

More than one patron gave Jean the up and down once over when she strolled past the lobby for the first time, heading for the conference area. Dressed fashionably, if in pieces one size too small for her voluptuous physique, Jean's face men would describe being not quite perfect; more sexy than pretty, and more raunchy than sexy. It stood her well in making play toys of much older men, as they in turn made a play toy of her. But she gave as good as she got with either men or women. These librarians were another matter, however. After Eric's comfortable reserve, the appearance of the teen for one of their functions is more than a bit disconcerting, especially for Miss Bostich.

"I see no one has set any fires yet," she whispered in a low but firm voice to an approaching Jean.

Jean smiled awkwardly, remembering the disapproval she received in Miss Bostich's eyes on her arrival. A look she expected from her boyfriend's mothers, sisters, and sometimes wives. She sighed deeply in her response, unintentionally accenting her chest even more.

"They are... a handful. It's not that I don't like kids..."

"Children, dear. We call them children here. Kids are the offspring of goats."

"Yes, ma'am. The ...'children'... I'm just not used to them. Not used to being around or alone with them." The silent plea in her voice. Even the disapproving librarian is a welcome comfort in this place.

"What about when you have children of your own, someday? Surely you've babysat for the practice and experience?" Miss Bostich knew full well from Jean's disarray that she did no such thing. Bostich's mind flitted rapidly with the kinds of things she imagined Jean did practice when younger – or now.

"Oh sure, I want kids sometime." She lied quickly. "But it's just that, I'm really not ready yet. Not married either," she put in quickly to gain some semblance of legitimacy in the librarian's view.

Jean helped yet another youngster to find the NASA website on one of the half-dozen PC terminals available in the room and showed her how to navigate to the robotics section. This whole affair was for show. A little public presence for the ARF. Goodwill. And perhaps a few donors to their nonprofit group would be found in the parents. Robotics clubs in high schools and colleges were flourishing in the early 21st century. Eric positioned the ARF to ride the wave as an ideal cover for their other, more illicit activities. Activities occasionally required him to sign in as a patron other than himself. Even the library issuing Eric his card did not have his true last name, any more than Jean. Layers of distance and protection were comforting.

Terribly easy hacking library user accounts. Using a borrowed card from a young admirer, it let Jean, the ARF's primary cracker, easily surf to a network T: drive and look for any text files with a simple search command. Within a half hour, Jean sorted the login IDs of every patron to sign in on that particular machine for the past 6 months. And copied them to an Excel sheet for sorting.

As a result, even though the administrator took the precaution of disabling the 3.5" floppy and CD drives, Jean walked out less than an hour after she first sat down with a USB flash drive copy of the login file. Apparently, the administrator didn't know how to disable the USB ports or needed them. The ARF now possessed eight or nine hundred IDs with which to log anonymously onto the internet. Eric would tell her how pleased he was that night when they lay together quietly in the dark. Jean would giggle about how easy it all was. Not a real hack at all. More like phishing. 'Security through obscurity' was a hacker's best friend.

An uneventful drive back to the compound. Jean drove in Europe since she was abandoned there in Holland by her math professor father at the tender age of 12. Making her way to England and returning to the US took her three long educational years.

A few pleasant moments were spent thinking of Eric. Their difference in ages made for raised eyebrows, as most of the other team members were nearly as young as Jean herself. When she thought of the only other graying head of the group, the retired physics teacher Nestor, she was saddened a bit. Not that she had any qualms about sleeping with a man old enough to be her grandfather, or shy about getting a response from him, but he was so damn comfortable to be around since she was recruited for the project. Quiet and intense, a being razor sharp that helped him keep this group of eclectic minds on a common track – and enjoy it in the process. She supposed she respected him. That must be it. A feeling not common for her to feel about men. Now, though, that keen intellect was hampered by Alzheimer's. It saddened her to think of it, but try as she would to find a happy thought on another topic, this wasn't her day.

She spent the rest of the drive back to the compound in a reflective mood she couldn't shake.

https://books2read.com/AliveBeDeemed

www.ingramcontent.com/pod-product-compliance
Lightning Source LLC
Chambersburg PA
CBHW030412310726
48979CB00002B/381

9798986489599